I0598300

Empty Hearts

By Sheila Claydon

Amazon Print ISBN 978-1-77362-584-3

Books We Love
A quality publisher of genre fiction.
Airdrie Alberta

Copyright 1985 by Sheila Claydon
Cover art by Michelle Lee

All rights reserved. Without limited the rights under copyright reserved above, no part of this publication may be reproduced, stored in or introduced into a retrieval system, or transmitted, in any form, or by any means (electronic, mechanical, photocopying, recording or otherwise) without the prior permission of both the copyright owner and the publisher of this book

* * *

Dedication

To the real Dirk Van Allen with many apologies for unwittingly stealing his name

Chapter One

1983

"Stop fooling, Eleanor, and hurry up!" Holly pushed a stack of paper to one side and perched on the edge of her friend's desk with a resigned sigh. "I should have known better than to arrive promptly for our lunch date; you've become a workaholic since you started this agency."

"I'm being completely serious." Eleanor Kingsman refused to be rushed as she opened a red folder and jabbed her finger at the first page. "Peter Van Allen, five years old; Father a member of the diplomatic staff at the British Embassy in Moscow. It's absolutely ideal."

"It most decidedly is not." Holly frowned in irritation. "When I said that I was thinking of visiting Moscow, I meant as a tourist."

"But what will staying at all the right hotels achieve? It certainly won't give you the insight you need for your book."

"And you think staying in the rarefied atmosphere of the British Embassy will I suppose."

Eleanor ignored the sarcasm. "It's the child, isn't it? If I'd offered you any other chance to work in Moscow, you'd have jumped at it; but you can't face the child."

"That's unfair, and from you of all people." The colour drained from Holly's face leaving two angry red spots high on her cheekbones. "I thought you understood."

"I do. That's why I'm offering the job to you instead of to one of my registered nannies." Eleanor closed the folder and leaned back in her chair, her grey eyes soft with sympathy. "You're not exactly short on experience, Holly, but until you bury the ghosts from your past you'll carry on wasting your talent."

* * *

Two weeks later, with Sheremetyevo Airport behind her, Holly approached central Moscow with a trepidation that was tiptoeing towards excitement. After all, the care of a five-year-old boy was a small price to pay for six months in the land of the Tsars, Tolstoy and Rachmaninov. And maybe Eleanor was right—maybe the job would help her come to terms with her own past so that she could start her life again.

She smiled faintly as she recalled her last days in London. Once she had agreed to take the job, Eleanor had not given her time to change her mind, but had immediately bullied her into a shopping spree, spending Holly's money freely as she persuaded her to buy a sheepskin jacket and a pair of warm boots, as well as sweaters and trousers and several woollen skirts.

"For goodness sake! I'm going to work as a nanny, not an Ambassador," she had grumbled as she added up the cost of her purchases.

"You'll get just as cold." Eleanor had ignored her protests and added a fur hat to the pile of clothes. "Anyway, it's more than time you renovated your wardrobe. You haven't bought anything new since—"

"Since Martin died." Holly had finished the sentence without flinching, and met her friend's gaze with a wry smile. "It's all right, you've achieved the impossible, you've prised me out of my shell. I'm actually looking forward to going to Moscow."

As relief flooded Eleanor's round face, Holly suddenly realised how much her friend had hated playing devil's advocate after two years of bearing the brunt of Holly's unhappiness without complaint and with little thanks. Filled with contrition, she hugged her.

"And dressed like this I shall be a force to be reckoned with. Even young Peter Van Allen won't dare defy me. I'll probably come back with enough material for a series of books instead of just one."

* * *

She had paid for the clothes with a confident flourish, but now the cold hand of fear clutched at her stomach and she closed her eyes. It was easy to be brave in London, to let Eleanor persuade her that this was the right thing to do, but driving silently through the streets of Moscow, past snow-scrapers cleaning the roads in a heavy mechanical ballet, she was forced to face up to the future. No more procrastination, no more talking about a nonexistent book, she would have to start picking up the pieces of her past. Nausea almost overwhelmed her. She wouldn't even be a good nanny because she wouldn't be able to offer the child any real affection. Peter Van Allen was just a means to an end—the laying of a ghost.

"Are you okay Miss Williams?" Stephen Andrews, the young man who had met her at the airport, looked across at her anxiously.

Holly jumped at the sound of his voice. She had forgotten about her companions: Stephen, tall, dark and bespectacled, and the silent, uniformed chauffeur. She answered with a flush of embarrassment, "I'm fine, just rather tired. It's been a long day."

He smiled sympathetically. "Never mind, we're almost at the apartment. And with Mr. Van Allen away and Peter asleep, you won't be disturbed until morning."

Her eyes widened in surprise. "Was Mr. Van Allen called away suddenly?" She could think of no other reason for her employer's absence when a stranger was arriving to take charge of his son.

Stephen shook his head. "He's often away, which is probably why Peter is so difficult."

"Difficult!" Holly turned her back on the night scene outside and concentrated. "What exactly do you mean by 'difficult'?"

"I'm guessing he didn't warn the agency then?" Stephen shook his head in mock disgust. "Not that I blame him. With Peter's track record, it would have probably sent a straitjacket instead of a nanny."

"But I'm not even a proper nanny," Holly wailed. "I only agreed to take the post because I wanted to learn about Moscow for a…a project I have in mind. The agency cleared it with Mr. Van Allen. Apparently he was pleased. He said Peter had outgrown nursemaids and that some cultural education would do him good. I assumed that to mean that I can take him to any of the various museums and places of interest that I particularly wish to see."

"Rather you than me. I'd as soon take Ivan the Terrible to a Women's Institute meeting."

"He can't be that bad." Holly smiled despite herself.

"He's worse." Stephen laughed aloud, his eyes twinkling in the light of the street lamps. Then he reached over and patted her hand. "But don't worry. I'll willingly rescue you on your free days, and do the rounds with you. In fact, I insist on it."

Holly allowed her hand to remain passively under his as the car drew to a halt, suddenly aware that she was a long way from London and, in view of Stephen's revelations about Peter Van Allen, probably in need of all the new friends she could muster.

* * *

Later, in the spacious bedroom she had been allocated, she wondered rather desperately about her young charge. Perhaps Stephen had been exaggerating; after all, he was still in his early twenties, so at an age when he thought small children were a nuisance. Peter Van Allen would probably turn out to be a perfectly normal five-year-old whose only problem was the fact that his father was often absent.

She paused in the act of stowing a sweater into a drawer, and frowned. His father was something else, though. Fancy leaving Peter to meet his new nanny alone. She tried to remember what Eleanor had told her about him.

"In his early thirties, and a widower for several years, Dirk Van Allen is a high flier in the Foreign Office with a long list of credits behind him already: for example, he's served on loan to the Treasury as an economic specialist, and he's recently completed a brief stint on secondment to the Bank of England. He's probably aiming at an Ambassadorship, and he's already served on the diplomatic staff in Greece."

Eleanor hadn't stopped there. She had produced several newspaper clippings torn from the gossip columns. They all featured a tall, fair-haired man attending first nights, film premieres and a few overpublicized parties, always with a different girl on his arm, each one beautiful or titled or famous—and occasionally, all three.

Holly had peered closely at the photographs. He looked as exotic as his unlikely name, the blurred newsprint failing to hide a Byronic profile made unexpectedly boyish by a flop of hair.

"Too handsome by half," she had dismissed him crisply. "I'm going to Moscow to work; to gather material for my long overdue book. I shan't have time for frivolities."

Eleanor had grinned at her. "I'll believe that when you return unscathed from six months of continuous charm."

Holly shrugged at the memory and pushed the drawer shut, her unpacking complete. It wasn't fair to judge him on a few newspaper clippings, and she didn't have enough strength left to worry; the activity of the past two weeks, combined with her recent journey, had taken their toll. She kicked off her shoes and padded across the bedroom to the adjoining bathroom with a sigh of relief. She would allow herself the luxury of a long, hot bath before claiming the bedtime drink that Mrs. Malpass, the housekeeper, had promised her.

* * *

When she returned to the bedroom twenty minutes later, she was pleasantly surprised to find her bedcovers turned back and a laden tray beside the bed. Mrs. Malpass was just leaving but she paused in the doorway as Holly emerged from the bathroom.

"I did knock, my dear, but you didn't hear me. I thought you could probably do with more than a hot drink after your journey, so I made toasted sandwiches."

"They look delicious," Holly said appreciatively as she removed a clean napkin from a pile of crusty brown sandwiches, "And please, I don't want to eat alone. If you have the time I'd love you to join me. There's so much I need to learn about the life here. And if you could tell me something about Peter too, I'd be glad. I know so little about him."

The housekeeper didn't need a second invitation, but as she closed the door and sank into an armchair, Holly sensed that a reluctance to be disloyal to her employer was warring with her natural inclination to gossip. Anxious not to offend, she steered the conversation on to safe ground for a while, discussing the daily routine of the household, and listening to a detailed account of Mr. Van Allen's culinary preferences, before leading the conversation back to Peter.

Eleanor had achieved more than she knew when she persuaded her friend to go to Moscow. Without being aware she was doing it, Holly instinctively began to use all the old skills that had once made her an extraordinarily successful interviewer and journalist. Trained to extract information painlessly, by the time she bade Mrs. Malpass

10

good night, she had found out all there was to know about Peter Van Allen.

What she had learned didn't please her, however, and she paid for her duplicity with a restless night. Until the early hours of the morning her dreams were vague, peopled with indeterminate shadows, but then they became black shapes moving against a background of leaping flames, and she was screaming, just as she had that night...

Something cold touched her face, dragging her back to consciousness, and she opened her eyes with a shudder. She could feel a cold sweat across her forehead and she was shivering uncontrollably, partly from fear, partly from despair. It was such a long time since she had last had the nightmare that she had thought she was over it and had discarded the dreamless security of her sleeping pills. Surely it wasn't going to recur now she was in a strange country, away from familiar doctors and sympathetic friends?

* * *

Now fully awake, she became aware that she wasn't alone. Fighting to control her still shaking body, she stared into the shadowy room. It was too dark to see properly but she knew it was Peter who stood watching her. He was motionless, his pyjamas a pale lozenge of grey topped by the white blur of his face. She tried to speak, to reassure him, knowing that her cries must have woken him, but her voice was no more than a croak, and by the time she had pushed herself up against the pillows and switched on the bedside light, he had gone.

She started to follow him but as she reached for her dressing-gown some warier instinct prevailed. If he had wanted to, he would have stayed. The speed and silence of his exit indicated just the opposite and she decided it was better to ignore the whole incident unless he chose to talk about it.

11

She knew she had made the right decision when she entered the dining-room the following morning. Peter gave a scowl that would have made a strong man quail.

"Hello." She helped herself to coffee and toast from the heated trolley and carried it across to the table.

He managed to eat his porridge, ignore her entirely and yet still convey intense dislike, all without lifting his eyes from the comic beside his plate. Holly paid no attention. If that was how he wanted to play it, she could outlast him. She rifled through several English newspapers folded neatly on the table and selected a tabloid for easy early morning assimilation.

It contained a lengthy article by one of her former colleagues and she read it with interest, becoming so engrossed that she forgot about the small boy sitting opposite her until he began to fidget.

"Have you finished?" She gave him a friendly smile as she sipped her coffee, then pulled a face. "Goodness, my coffee is almost cold. I was so busy reading that I forgot about my breakfast."

He pushed his spoon round his messy bowl. "If I do that with my porridge, Malpy gets cross and makes me eat it, even when it's really cold."

"I expect that's because she has gone to a lot of trouble to cook it for you." Holly put her paper aside and concentrated on her toast, keeping her voice casual and relaxed.

"Mmm." He grudgingly conceded the point, raising his eyes to stare at her.

She smiled and pressed home. "I expect she wants to be sure you are eating enough while your father is away."

As soon as she mentioned his father the black eyes flashed and he pushed his bowl away with an angry hand, shooting a large globule of porridge onto the table where it congealed into a glutinous grey mess.

"You'd better fetch a cloth," she said, reaching casually for her paper while she inwardly cursed herself for her insensitivity.

12

He ignored her and turned a page of his comic.

"Peter." The voice from the doorway startled them both. "Miss Williams asked you to fetch a cloth so I suggest you do just that."

"Yes, Father." For an instant Peter's eyes brightened as he looked at the tall figure who had just entered the dining-room, but then the sullen frown returned and he climbed down from his chair and stalked from the room without another word.

"Peter needs a firm hand, Miss Williams." Dirk Van Allen strode across to the trolley and poured himself some coffee. "So may I suggest that reading at the breakfast table is hardly likely to promote the good manners I would like you to instill in him."

Holly swallowed her angry retort. She had to admit that, to an outsider, a breakfast table strewn with pages of her newspaper and decorated with a sticky blob of porridge must look very slovenly.

"I'm sorry," she managed, a flush suffusing her normally pale cheeks. "I didn't want to start off on the wrong foot with a lot of rules and regulations; I thought it was more important to get to know him first."

Dirk Van Allen didn't answer her directly, merely gave a nod of acknowledgement as he started to sit down. Then the sight of the congealed mess in Peter's breakfast bowl caught his attention and, with a look of distaste, he indicated the door.

"If you've finished your breakfast, perhaps you'd be good enough to join me in my study. I haven't much time and I would like us to discuss Peter undisturbed."

Without waiting for an answer, he turned away. Leaving her toast unfinished, Holly grabbed her coffee cup and followed him. He led the way down the main corridor of the apartment to a door at the far end, and then stood aside, waiting for her to enter. She tilted her chin proudly and walked past him. He needn't think he was going to

13

bully her. If she was good enough to take charge of his son, then she deserved the courtesy of an explanation.

"I wasn't expecting to see you so soon," she challenged him straight away. "I understood from Mrs. Malpass that you were to be away until Sunday."

"A change of plans." He raised an eyebrow as he set his coffee cup on the desk, surprised by the intensity in her voice. "An unscheduled meeting has brought me back to Moscow and as I have ten minutes to spare before it starts, now seems as good a time as any to fill you in on your responsibilities."

Ten minutes! Holly stared at him. Ten minutes to hand his son over to a stranger. No wonder the child was difficult.

Her disapproval must have shown because Dirk Van Allen waved her to a chair with a bitter laugh. "You obviously think I'm a very unnatural parent, Miss Williams, but the truth is that you are the fourth nanny I've employed in as many months, so the novelty is beginning to wear a little thin."

"Who frightened them away, you or Peter?" The words were out before Holly could stop herself, but to her relief he smiled.

"Touché. And I apologise for my abrupt entry this morning. Possibly there was a method to your approach that I failed to appreciate."

"I doubt it." Holly relaxed slightly and met his gaze. "I'm not a trained nanny, Mr. Van Allen, although I do have some experience of small boys. And while I'm in Moscow I intend to pursue some historical research— within the confines of my responsibilities to Peter, of course," she added hastily. "I believe the agency explained everything."

"They also gave you an excellent reference." He studied her over the rim of his cup. "You're more than welcome to introduce Peter to his Russian heritage. It might even do him some good."

"I thought you were English," Holly said, frowning.

14

"I am." Suddenly Dirk Van Allen's tone was clipped, almost angry. "His mother was half-Russian though; half-Russian and half-Italian, an uneasy combination. Peter seems to have inherited her temperament." He rose abruptly, as if his few brief words had explained his son, and walked across to the window.

Holly watched him curiously, wondering if Peter had inherited his mother's looks as well, because he bore no resemblance to his father. Dirk Van Allen was tall, well over six feet, and the newspapers hadn't done justice to his blond good looks, which were enhanced by deep hazel eyes, watchful and alert behind a thick fringe of lashes. He was extraordinarily attractive and, judging from his casual confidence, well aware of it. Peter's tiny, birdlike frame and snapping black eyes, though appealing, were very different.

"Does Peter remember his mother? I mean, should I refer to her or will it upset him...?" Her voice trailed off in embarrassment as Dirk turned from the window. His eyes were unexpectedly cold and she sensed that he had to force out his answer.

"He doesn't remember her. She died soon after he was born."

"I'm sorry. It must have been very difficult for you," Holly murmured, wondering why her question had upset him so badly. After all, if the press cuttings were to be believed, he hadn't ever behaved like a grieving widower.

As if he read her thoughts, he left the window and dropped into the swivel chair behind his desk, long legs askew as he swung towards her.

"I sense your disapproval, Miss Williams. Don't I live up to your expectations of what a father should be? Am I too hard? Too unfeeling?"

"I have hardly been here long enough to make a judgment," Holly protested, surprised and flustered by his sudden attack.

15

"Precisely!" The hazel eyes which had glinted with sardonic humour only moments earlier, suddenly hardened. "You are here to care for Peter, not question his relationship with me. If you have any disciplinary problems let me know—otherwise, he's in your sole charge. Understood?"

"Perfectly." Holly stood up, anticipating dismissal. A dull flush of anger coloured her face. How dare he speak to her like that. No wonder Peter's other nannies had left.

"I'll be home by about eight tonight," Dirk continued, leaning back in his chair and folding his arms. "Peter will already be in bed, of course, but I'd like you to join me for dinner so that we can continue our discussion."

"That won't be necessary." Holly stood stiffly, her eyes riveted on a spot slightly above his head. "I'm sure Mrs. Malpass can fill me in on any details."

"I must insist." The deep voice brooked no argument. "There are several matters to settle and, as you will be part of the household for the next few months, I think we should get to know one another a little, if only for Peter's sake."

Holly could see the sense behind his remarks. With Peter their shared responsibility, they had to make some effort, however tedious it might be for both of them.

"Perhaps you'd be kind enough to ask Mrs. Malpass to serve dinner at eight-thirty?" he added.

"As you wish." Holly nodded stiffly as she swept past him. Once in the corridor, she remembered Mrs. Malpass' remarks of the night before.

"Mr. Van Allen can be very awkward, dear, and cold. Even Peter understands that. Why, I've often heard that child cry himself to sleep—but he won't let me near him. He curls into his bed like a sick animal and won't answer to anyone. What he needs is a mother, poor little scrap. But while Mr. Van Allen has a certain reputation with the ladies—if you take my meaning—there's never anyone permanent."

She had caught the housekeeper's meaning only too well and it didn't exactly endear her employer to her. She

16

wondered again about his wife. How had she lived with such coldness?

As if in answer to her question, she caught a beckoning flash of red through a half-open door. It led her into a sitting-room where a deep claret carpet and heavy curtains complemented the dress of a woman in a full-length portrait.

Holly's breath caught in her throat as she stepped into the room, mesmerised by the brilliant eyes staring out from the canvas. Black—blacker even than Peter's—and full of fire, they surveyed the room above a mouth the colour of ripe cherries. Long black curls cascaded over white shoulders, and the figure beneath the painted brocade of the vivid dress was exquisite.

'Isabella Vittorio, aged twenty-one,' she read on the small engraved plaque set in the frame. Although the name meant nothing to her, she knew, without being told, that this was a portrait of Peter's mother, Dirk Van Allen's dead wife, painted before he married her. She had never seen a more beautiful woman.

A shudder ran through her. Like her, Dirk Van Allen had lost too much. His constant affairs were a diversion from emotions too painful to contemplate. Peter's resemblance to his dead mother was probably the reason for his father's apparent coldness. His dark features must act like salt in an open wound, withholding acceptance of the past, never allowing Dirk to forget.

Isabella Vittorio's face dissolved into a blur as Holy remembered her own loss and tears misted her eyes. Hastily she turned away, blowing her nose hard on a tissue. Tears still came too easily at times, and she didn't want to confront Peter with swollen eyes.

Dirk Van Allen was standing in the doorway, watching her, and she jumped as she noticed him.

"I didn't hear you," Holly stammered and then, when he remained silent, she gestured towards the portrait. "She was very beautiful," she said in a high, unnatural voice.

17

"She was the toast of three cities." His voice was calm, almost disinterested, but Holly knew how much it cost him to speak because, as he glanced up at the portrait, his eyes held the same shuttered look as Peter's had at the breakfast table. The likeness between him and his son, despite their different colouring, was momentarily startling.

Chapter Two

Holly found Peter in the kitchen with Mrs. Malpass. He was scrubbing at a piece of paper with a stubby paintbrush.

"That looks exciting," she said in an interested voice.

"It's a storm." He didn't look up as he dug his brush deeper into the paper, making it soggy and pitted with his efforts.

"Are you going to paint some lightning?"

"It isn't that sort of storm." His voice was unfriendly as he added another swirl of paint to the almost completely black picture, spattering some of it across her hand.

She rubbed at it with a tissue and then reached for a fresh piece of paper. "Do you mind if I paint a picture too?"

He didn't look up but pushed an even stubbier paintbrush in her direction. With a feeling of relief, she began mixing colours. At least he was communicating.

She worked in silence for some minutes, expanding her picture colour by colour, from a stark outline of dark rocks to lowering grey clouds tinged with purple, and jagged slashes of bright yellow lightning. Then she added the white flash of breakers tossed by the storm and, aware that Peter was taking furtive peeps, the tilted prow of a sinking ship, its scarlet sail tattered by the wind. Finally she put down her brush and regarded her handiwork with satisfaction. It was crude, but it had movement and colour. She looked across at Peter.

"Go on," he said, his own work forgotten.

"I've finished." Holly turned the picture around so that he could look at it.

"There aren't any sailors."

Holly gave an exaggerated sigh. "I'm not very good at painting people. Why don't you do it?"

After a moment's hesitation, he jabbed his brush into the inevitable black paint and daubed the outline of a man, arms outstretched, on the tilting deck. Then he added two more in the water, and what looked like a box being washed up on the beach.

Ignoring the fact that each man was taller than the main mast, Holly entered the game.

"Wreckers," she said, and painted an ominous shadow in the foreground, a huge hand holding an oversized lamp. "And there would be a fire to trick the sailors; let's use red and orange and yellow because it will have to be a very bright fire to lead the ship ashore. Here, let me show you." She streaked a corner of the page with red. "Now, you add some yellow and orange. Look, the flames are getting higher."

"A real bonfire!"

Hearing the satisfaction in his voice, and seeing him happily absorbed, Holly left the table and rinsed her hands at the sink. Mrs. Malpass was buttoning herself into a shapeless fur coat, nodding approvingly all the while.

"You've done better than the last one already. He wouldn't talk to her at all."

"Beginner's luck," Holly smiled at her and then turned back to the table as she left the kitchen.

Peter was still concentrating on the picture, the corner of his tongue peeping from his mouth, his lashes a thick sweep of black against his pale cheeks. Holly's heart contracted. Martin would have looked like that now. Fairer of course, and taller, but with the same rapt concentration... No! She mustn't think of him. She'd spent two years schooling herself not to remember.

Forcing a smile, she asked, "How is it coming along?" But when she saw what he was doing to the painting, her face filled with horror.

20

Peter didn't notice. Instead he continued to add flames to the picture, building up the fire until it engulfed the sea and the rocks. Even the clouds disappeared as he slashed bright paint across them. It was like the return of her nightmare, shocking in its vividness, dangerously close to her own painful memories.

"Don't!" She pulled the brush from his hand before she could stop herself, voice shrill, hands clammy.

Peter stared at her, his eyes filling with resentment. "Just because you don't want me to spoil your silly old picture."

"No, it's not that." Holly tried to pull herself together. "Here, paint something else," she suggested, holding out the brush. "Paint a picture of the treasure the wreckers found."

"No." Peter's black eyes were stony as he ignored her outstretched hand. "The fire burned it up." Then, when she didn't respond, he deliberately picked up a pot of red paint and dropped it on to the floor where it spattered, blood-like, across the tiles, and sprayed her shoes.

Tears sprang to Holly's eyes. She had failed already. By letting her memories take over she had earned Peter's animosity instead of his trust. Eleanor had been wrong to persuade her, stupid to think that she could cope. When Dirk Van Allen returned she would sort out things with him. She would pay the cost of her flight, of course, but she would explain why it couldn't work and leave as soon as possible.

She could hear the satisfaction in Peter's voice as he stared at her. "You're crying. I never cry."

"I'm not really crying." She rubbed her hands across her eyes, wondering how she could best explain her behaviour. "Not about the picture anyway."

"The paint then." He was determined to take the blame. "It's all over your shoes."

Holly stared down at her feet in despair. She didn't want Peter to think he had reduced her to tears over such a trifle. It would become another weapon in his armoury, along with the silence and the defiance. But she couldn't tell him about Martin.

"Peter, are you responsible for this mess?" Dirk Van Allen's voice cut across her confusion.

"Yes, Father." The flush of triumph faded from Peter's face, leaving him as pale as Holly.

"Then I suggest that you clean it up." Dirk took a damp cloth from the sink and tossed it on to the floor. "And start with Miss William's shoes."

The coldness in his voice brought Holly to her senses. "Really, it's all right," she protested. "It was an accident— I'll clear it up."

"Sit down." Dirk ignored her pleas and pushed a chair in her direction. "You look upset. Has Peter been giving you a bad time?"

"No...he...that is, we were painting." Holly subsided into the chair while Peter tried to rub the paint from her shoes. "And it was as much my fault as Peter's that the paint was spilt."

She could see that he didn't believe her but, faced with her cool gaze, he refrained from further comment. Instead he plugged in the electric kettle. "I'll make us both some coffee. My meeting was unexpectedly brief and as I wasn't expecting to be in Moscow today, I'm at a bit of a loose end."

"That must be annoying." Holly deftly removed the cloth from Peter's paint-stained fingers and began to mop up the floor while Dirk's back was turned.

"On the contrary," he replied, spooning coffee into two mugs, "it will give me time to tackle a long overdue report. You don't type by any chance, do you?"

"Yes, I do." Holly answered automatically as she handed the cloth back to Peter and pushed him gently towards the sink.

"Then you can work for me this morning; type the first draft of my report. It will be good for your research because it's about Moscow and how Russian society is changing."

22

"But who will look after Peter?" Holly was too startled by his assumption that she would do whatever he asked to offer more than a token protest.

"Oh, he can stay with Mrs. Malpass. She'll find something for him to do, or if she's busy then he can bring a book and sit with you."

The note of impatience in his voice appalled Holly. Dirk Van Allen didn't care about his son. She wondered if he even liked him. Her maternal instincts, thwarted for too long, began to surface as she glanced across at Peter. He was kneeling on a stool beside the sink, trying to wash the streaks of paint from his fingers. He didn't appear to be listening to their conversation but his face looked pinched and thin.

She made a frantic mental resume of her scanty knowledge of the city's landmarks. "I'm sorry but I can't help you because I already have plans for today. Peter and I are going to Gorky Park." Surely that was a place likely to interest a small boy.

Two pairs of eyes stared at her in disbelief.

Dirk, clearly irritated by her independence, was dismissive. "You can take him to Gorky Park another day."

"But I'd be breaking a promise." Holly didn't look at Peter as she joined him at the sink and plunged her hands into the soapy water. Instead, she wondered why she was fighting for him when only minutes earlier she had been planning to escape.

"He understands about deadlines and overdue reports, don't you Peter?" Unexpectedly, Dirk included his son in the conversation, speaking to him as if he were an adult.

"Yes, Father." Peter's voice was dead, his eyes blank as he carefully replaced the soap in the dish. The cool little reply stabbed at Holly. How many times had he been pushed to one side; made to feel a nuisance? She couldn't easily refuse to do Dirk Van Allen's typing, especially as he had said it would be useful for her research, but she could make him pay for his unkindness to his small son.

"Perhaps you could take Peter to the park yourself while I type your report," she said innocently.

Dirk's eyes rounded in surprise. He obviously wasn't used to having his orders questioned.

"I'm afraid that's impossible. I shall be busy all day."

"Well, tomorrow then. Surely you have free time on a Saturday," Holly persisted, not sure why she was jeopardising her job but determined to win a concession for Peter.

Dirk's face darkened and she knew he was about to make a curt refusal. In desperation, she turned to Peter.

"You'd like that, wouldn't you? You'd like your father to take you to Gorky Park tomorrow."

"Could we skate?" The disbelief in Peter's eyes had vanished and they were bright with anticipation. He was too young to follow the undercurrents of the conversation and heard only that his father was going to spend time with him. Dirk noticed his excitement and the curt disclaimer Holly half-expected never came.

"Very well, Miss Williams," he said in a dangerously soft voice. "If you type my report today, we will *all* go to Gorky Park tomorrow. Now are you satisfied?"

* * *

At one o'clock that afternoon, Holly pulled the last sheet of paper from the typewriter with a sigh of relief. The report had indeed given her an insight into contemporary Moscow that would complement her historical research and she wished she could question Dirk about it. It had seemed wiser to remain silent and concentrate instead on her typing, however, with an occasional check on Peter who had fallen asleep in a corner of the study with a picture book on his lap.

Dirk, totally absorbed in a pile of paperwork, appeared to have forgotten them both. Against the enveloping gloom of the day, his hair shone bright gold beneath the light of the desk lamp.

Holly watched him curiously, wondering about his animosity towards Peter. Why should he so dislike his own child? Had Peter been the cause of his mother's death; his birth too much for her? Or perhaps was it the likeness that he found so hard to bear; was Peter a constant and painful reminder.

As if she had spoken her questions aloud, Dirk suddenly looked up and their eyes met.

"I've finished." Holly cleared her throat of an awkward huskiness. "Is there anything else?"

"Only lunch."

"In that case, I'll go and warn Mrs. Malpass," she said, anxious to escape from the disturbing hazel eyes, their irises black ringed and lynx-like. That was what he reminded her of—a beautiful, merciless hunter. She shivered as she pushed back her chair.

He reached the door first, his lazy movements deceptively fast. "We'll go together."

The eyes were closer now, and she noticed specks of gold in them. His mouth was close, too, and curved in a humourless smile that made her unaccountably nervous. She turned from the doorway with a forced exclamation.

"We nearly forgot Peter. I'd better wake him."

"Don't bother." Dirk's hand circled her wrist, preventing her from rousing the sleeping child. "He often wakes during the night and then cat-naps in the day. Mrs. Malpass will save his lunch."

Remembering Peter's night-time visit to her room she nodded reluctantly. "I suppose that would be best. Perhaps I'd better wait, too, until he wakes."

"Are you trying to avoid spending time with me, Miss Williams." Dirk's voice was scornful.

Holly jerked her arm away. "Of course not. I was just thinking of Peter."

"In that case, there's no problem." He took a light blanket from the cushioned window-seat and draped it around his son. "Peter will be fine here while we eat, and you can return for him after lunch while I tackle the rest of my paperwork. After all, I have to be free for Gorky Park tomorrow don't I?"

He laughed as Holly flushed pink, but when their eyes met she knew that despite his light manner, he hadn't forgiven her for her interference and intended to exact every ounce of retribution possible.

* * *

Mrs. Malpass was stirring a large pan of thick soup when they entered the kitchen. She turned to them with a smile.

"I was just coming to see if you were ready," she said, dishing out three bowlfuls before cutting thick slices of bread from a freshly baked loaf. She nodded understandingly when Holly explained about Peter.

"He can have his later then, poor lamb. He's been looking very peaky lately."

If Dirk noticed the implied criticism in her comment, he ignored it. Instead, he pulled a bowl of soup towards him and took a hunk of bread, indicating that Holly should do the same.

Mrs. Malpass stared at him in disbelief, her own lunch untouched. Holly noticed the solitary tray on a corner of the kitchen table. It was set with silverware and a napkin. It was obvious that Dirk usually ate alone.

"I didn't want to wake Peter so I've decided to join you and Miss Williams in the kitchen instead of eating off a tray in the study. You don't mind, do you?" Dirk turned up the wattage of his smile as he spoke to the housekeeper.

"Of course I don't mind." Mrs. Malpass bridled slightly before glancing suspiciously at Holly. "It's just unusual, that's all."

"And very cozy too. Now that I know what I've been missing, I might do it more often." Dirk's face was bland and friendly. Only Holly recognised the threat behind his

26

words. He was going to pay her back for standing up to him by inflicting himself on her as often as possible.

* * *

The afternoon left her little time to brood, however. Peter woke from his sleep in a fractious mood and his demands were peremptory. "What are we going to do this afternoon?"

"I hadn't thought. What would you like to do?" Holly asked him.

"Can we do anything?" He challenged her.

"It depends what you have in mind."

"The zoo museum," came the swift reply.

Holly's heart sank. It was the last thing she felt like doing, rows of stuffed animals being low down on her list of interests, but Peter was her responsibility after all. The sooner she won his trust, the sooner she could help him understand his father. The thought startled her, coming out of nowhere as it did. Why should she feel responsible for rectifying their troubled relationship? How ridiculous. She pushed the idea aside and smiled at Peter.

"Should I call a taxi? I don't know my way around Moscow yet."

"I know the way to the zoo museum," Peter said proudly, giving her his first genuine smile. "We can walk there very quickly."

Holly looked doubtfully at the grey sky outside and tried for a reprieve. "It looks awfully cold and dreary. Don't you think we should wait for a better day?"

"You said anywhere!" He stuck out his bottom lip.

"Well, all right, but let me check with Mrs. Malpass first." Nothing would induce her to speak to Dirk who was now working quietly in his study.

"He must know the way blindfold by now," the housekeeper replied to Holly's anxious question. "Although why he likes all those dead animals, I can't imagine. You'll be safe enough with Peter, my dear, and if you do get lost just go to the nearest Metro. There's a push button map on the wall of every station, and if you call up your destination—it's Biblioteka Imenilenina for this apartment—the route will light up. Have you enough money?"

"Yes." Holly smiled her thanks as she remembered the complicated business of exchanging sterling for roubles at the airport on her arrival. She hadn't expected to need it so soon—but then neither had she expected that her first view of Moscow, the city that had so fascinated her during her political and historical studies at university, would be in the company of a stranger's five-year-old son.

* * *

Peter was waiting, bright-eyed and expectant, when she emerged from her bedroom.

"Come on." He pushed open the outer door impatiently and led her down a flight of stairs to a back entrance. She knew, from Stephen's remarks on the journey from the airport, that the apartment building had once been the property of a wealthy merchant, but Peter didn't give her time to admire the architecture. Instead, he hurried her through the door and down a maze of side streets. It wasn't until they reached the Serafimovicha Ulita that she gained her first real view of the red brick Kremlin with its well-known silhouette of thrusting cupolas and towers.

A sudden excitement gripped her. This was a part of the Russia she had come to see: The Kremlin, the fortress that was once the whole of Moscow. Beside it the curving Moscow River, an artery of trade since the Middle Ages, wound between the tall buildings like a silver ribbon. She recalled the tales of the Moscow Princes and their struggles against the Mongols, and later the Tartars. It was material which she wanted to embroider into a novel, vivid and compelling, the history of a country's struggle for survival.

28

"Hurry up." Peter interrupted her thoughts. "I want to show you the birds."

"Do you like them best?"

He nodded, not bothering to waste his breath on an answer, and before long they were climbing the steep incline of Herzen Street. The prospect changed almost immediately and Holly recognised settings from War and Peace in the tangle of lanes and tree-lined streets. A statue of Tchaikovsky heralded the Tchaikovsky Conservatoire and she paused breathlessly before it, remembering the great names of those who had studied there: Rachmaninov, Rostropovich, Khachaturian… But Peter urged her on, ignoring the unique railings patterned in the shapes of musical notes, and diving instead into the tall building that housed his beloved specimens.

* * *

By the time they left the museum, despite feeling slightly uneasy about Peter's enthusiasm for all things stuffed, Holly felt satisfied with her afternoon's work. Although she could hardly term their relationship friendly, he was at least talking to her; had in fact chattered incessantly as she trailed him round the exhibits.

She took a deep breath as they stepped outside, descending steps now powdered with a white frosting of snow. The air had become a lot colder and, despite her warm coat, she shivered.

"We'd better hurry," she warned Peter. "The snow is getting heavier."

He didn't answer but plodded along beside her, seemingly lost in his own thoughts, so she was surprised and pleased when his hand crept into hers as they made their way down an underground walkway. She looked down at him and was rewarded with a smile of such piercing sweetness that she was reminded briefly of the expression on Dirk's face at lunchtime when he had deliberately charmed Mrs. Malpass. She pushed the thought away. Time enough to think of him at dinner.

"I expect you're hungry," she said, squeezing Peter's fingers sympathetically. "What do you usually have for tea?"

Instead of answering he asked her a question of his own. "What is your real name? Not Miss Williams, the other one."

"It's a bit silly—it's Holly."

"Holly." he tried it several times. "I like it. May I call you Holly?"

"My friends usually do." It was strange but she felt as if the warmth from their clasped hands was creeping upwards, through her arm into her heart, melting the coldness that had been part of her for so long. Was this why Eleanor had persuaded her to come to Moscow? The sudden tears froze against her cheeks and she blinked them away, shivering in a sudden blast of Arctic wind.

"Come on, let's run." She tightened her grip and pulled him after her, old despair mingling with unexpected elation as they ran, hand in hand, through the rear door of the apartment block—and straight into Dirk.

The door caught him a glancing blow on the shoulder and he staggered slightly before scowling down at them.

"Do you usually enter buildings like this, or was it a momentary whim?"

"I'm sorry." Holly blushed scarlet. "We...it was cold outside."

He continued to look irritated as he turned his attention to his son. "I've lost count of the times I've told you not to run in the corridors Peter."

"I'm sorry, Father." Peter released Holly's hand and stood, rigid with tension, just inside the door.

"See that it doesn't happen again." Dirk, ignoring his apology, directed his remark at Holly before jamming a hat on his head and striding out into the night, leaving the door swinging behind him.

Cheeks scarlet with indignation, Holly led Peter upstairs, forcing enthusiasm into her voice as she talked about the tea that would be waiting for him. She wasn't going to let Dirk's unreasonable anger spoil her tenuous friendship with his son, who was now ominously silent.

* * *

Mrs. Malpass opened the door with a cheerful smile, then left them to hang their coats on hooks in the hall while she returned to the kitchen. Holly stared down at the little boy as he struggled with his boots, and tried to shake off a sudden wave of depression. Perhaps it would be better after all to keep to her earlier decision to leave Moscow and return to London before any lasting damage was done. If she stayed she knew that her relationship with Dirk would be stormy because she would be unable to stand aside and ignore his treatment of his son. Better, perhaps, if she withdrew now before the question of Peter's welfare became a battleground between them.

Peter finally managed to remove his boots and, scowling, kicked them out of sight beneath the hall-stand. Holly refrained from comment. Now wasn't the time to remind him that his boots belonged in the kitchen where the old-fashioned radiator would dry them. Instead, she dropped a casual hand on his shoulder and directed him towards the dining-room.

He sat silently at the table, making no attempt to eat the boiled egg in its Humpty-dumpty eggcup.

"Come on." Holly picked up his spoon and scooped out some rich, yellow yolk. "I once knew a little girl who didn't like eggs, and her grandmother gave her a magic eggcup that turned the egg yolk into whatever flavour she chose." She began to tell him one of Martin's favourite stories, pushing away memories of her own dead son's eager voice and concentrating on the downcast face in front of her instead. Peter, however, wasn't listening.

31

Suddenly he pushed the egg away and looked at her, his face dark with despair. "Now we won't be able to go to Gorky Park." His voice was hard and not at all childlike. "He won't take me now I've been naughty."

"Your father won't cancel the trip to Gorky Park for such a small thing as running in the corridor Peter, and anyway I'll tell him it was my fault because I suggested it, didn't I?"

Peter accepted another spoonful of egg with obvious relief, his five-year-old mind prepared to believe her. Holly pushed her own doubts to the back of her mind. They would have to be faced when she had dinner with Dirk, but right now she had to get the bleak expression out of Peter's eyes. She returned to the story of the magic eggcup, and watched his face slowly become rapt with concentration. When she finished he remained wide-eyed and thoughtful for a long time and she suddenly realised that he was savouring each word, imprinting it on his memory in case he never heard it again.

Anger surged through her. Despite his expensive clothes and well-cut hair, he was deprived in a way poor children from a caring home never were; deprived of loving attention and continuity, so that even a story was an event in his lonely little life.

For the first time since Martin's death all her feelings were directed outside herself. Peter needed her, needed someone to stand between him and his father, and, in some strange way, she needed him. She wouldn't think about leaving Moscow again, whatever the cost to herself, until she had forced Dirk Van Allen to become a proper father.

She knew that she was probably tackling the impossible, but she also knew that it was the only way she would finally lay Martin's ghost. If she could give Peter the father her own son had never had, she might be able to face the future again. She might even learn to live with the past.

* * *

"I was beginning to think you had forgotten our dinner date." Sarcasm edged Dirk's voice as he indicated a tray of drinks on a small side table.

"I'd like a dry sherry please." Holly ignored his tone and sank gracefully into the soft cushions of the sofa. Then, as he handed her a brimming glass, she remarked upon the decor of the sitting-room, the weather, her afternoon with Peter—letting the subjects flow, so that Dirk was forced to respond with social pleasantries until Mrs. Malpass announced that their meal was ready.

If he was angry at her ploy he didn't comment. Instead he related several anecdotes about his own day, so that by the time they faced each other across the table, Holly was beginning to feel more confident.

After putting Peter to bed at seven-thirty, she had soaked for too long in the bath a she plotted the gradual erosion of Dirk's defences. She knew from her own experience how grief could take over every waking hour, turning the mind inward on itself until everything in life became dull and flat. She remembered how, when she herself had been at her lowest ebb, her doctor had persuaded her to become a hospital visitor. It hadn't been a cure, but the hours in the stark hospital wards had taken her out of herself, offered her a tiny hold on life, a bridge to the rest of the human race. Well, Dirk Van Allen was going to cross that bridge if she had anything to do with it. He was going to acknowledge the depression that he hid so well, that only a fellow sufferer would recognise, and become a volunteer visitor into the life of his son. Starting with the proposed trip to Gorky Park.

She knew, however, that the transformation would be far from easy. He was too autocratic to take kindly to obvious manipulation so she would have to find his weak spot, his Achilles heel. It wasn't until the bath water had become uncomfortably cool that she realised she had had the solution all along. Dirk Van Allen had only one weakness—a taste for pretty women. And whatever her

33

other failings, Holly knew she was pretty. She didn't possess the sensual beauty of his dead wife, but she was attractive enough to turn heads when she entered a room.

Her own disastrous marriage at the age of nineteen had left her impervious to men in general, and to the cold arrogance of someone like Dirk Van Allen in particular, but she could act, couldn't she? Television journalism had taught her to project the right image. If Dirk could only be reached through feminine wiles, then she would produce them. Not enough to cause problems—just enough to keep him interested, to make him want to spend time with her, and consequently, with Peter.

Satisfied with her decision, she had stepped from the bath and dried herself vigorously before selecting a soft wool dress that enhanced her slender curves. Then, sweeping her shoulder-length hair up into a loose knot, she had coaxed feathery tendrils at her temples, and enhanced her pale complexion with blusher high on her cheekbones and a deep rose pink lipstick. Her eyes were naturally large and dark but she had brushed a trace of green shadow on to the lids and thickened her lashes with mascara. Then, with a final glance in the mirror, she had taken a deep breath and swept along the corridor to the sitting-room.

Dirk had handed her the sherry with a faint smile, his eyes sweeping from the studied disarray of her brown curls to the revealing folds of her dress. Steeling herself against the intrusive intimacy of his gaze, she had smiled sweetly, letting her fingers brush against his as she reached for the glass. Now, sitting opposite him at the polished dining table and trying to do justice to an excellent steak, she was satisfied that her ruse was working.

She looked at him, trying to judge his mood, wondering how soon she could broach the subject of Gorky Park.

"*Mir i druzba!*" He raised his wine glass in a toast, his eyes shadowed and unfathomable. "It's a Russian greeting—peace and friendship," he explained with a smile.

"*Mir i druzba!*" Holly repeated solemnly.

34

For a long moment they stared at one another as a current of tension began to flow between them, unexpected and dangerous, warning Holly that she might soon find herself out of her depth. She scrambled for the shallows, using flippancy to distract him.

"We'll need peace and friendship if we're to survive an afternoon's skating together tomorrow. I've never skated in my life."

The tension shattered with his answering laughter and when Mrs. Malpass returned with their dessert they were discussing the proposed itinerary for the following day.

The housekeeper looked surprised as she listened to their plans, but she made no comment other than a promise to prepare a late lunch so that they could enjoy the best hours of daylight. Holly, however, detected a faint air of disapproval. Mrs. Malpass had obviously noticed her changed manner and was inclined to believe the worst. She thought Holly was deliberately setting her cap at her employer.

Well, she could hardly be blamed for thinking that when it was exactly what Holly was doing—even if it was for the best possible reasons. Although she was sorry to lose the confidence of her new friend so quickly, she wasn't going to allow her personal feelings to stand in the way of reconciliation between Dirk and his son. It was suddenly the most important thing in her life, more important even than her proposed book or her journalistic reputation. Bringing Dirk and Peter together would mean that something good had grown from her own blighted life.

She reached for her wine glass again and sipped the ruby red Mukuzani with enjoyment. Dirk had explained its Georgian origin when he poured it, and she liked its fresh, dry flavour.

He nodded approvingly as he topped up her glass. "You like our Russian cuisine?"

"So far." She smiled brightly. "Though I detect a distinctly British influence?"

He laughed. "Mrs. Malpass has lived in Russia for a very long time so her food is a highly original mixture of two cultures."

"How long has she worked for you?" Holly was curious about his life, anxious to learn the full history of Peter's home background.

"Only since I came to Moscow. She's an embassy employee." Dirk pushed his plate aside and reached for the wine again.

"Is it usual for the embassy to provide staff, I mean in diplomatic circles?" Holly began to probe, using subtle body language to distract him from the purpose behind her questioning.

"I wouldn't know." Did she detect a flicker of amusement in his answer, as if he had decided to play her at her own game? She flashed him a quick glance from under her lashes and noticed a glint in his eye, although his words were matter-of-fact when he answered.

"Each embassy has its own rules, and because I'm a relative newcomer I don't know all of Moscow's specific customs. Actually, it's obvious that I still have a lot to learn if I'm ever to make it as a successful diplomat when even you saw that I'm more likely to start wars than avoid them within three minutes of meeting me."

"I did not." Holly flushed uncomfortably, remembering their first meeting and her indignant remarks. "I merely suggested…"

"I know exactly what you suggested." Suddenly his face looked grave. "And you are probably right. I'm not always an easy person to live with, and neither is Peter. Together we make a fairly explosive combination."

He finished his rather surprising statement on a questioning note and Holly laughed, relieved at his relaxed manner and encouraged by his flirtatious attitude.

"I expect I can manage. I come from a fairly temperamental background myself." With an inward shudder, she remembered her three brothers and their rock band. It seemed a lifetime ago; the excitement of trying to

36

establish themselves on the music scene, the intolerable tension when things were going badly. Even when Darren had taken them over, with his big ideas and easy money, it had still been difficult. She had coped until she was pregnant, fitting herself round their demanding schedule, playing down her own talents, going without sleep to be with them. She had even tried to ignore the evidence of Darren's faithlessness as she drove down empty motorways at three in the morning, prepared to do almost anything to save her marriage.

For a moment the remembered strain shadowed her face, but she continued with an effort, "My brothers are all musicians, quite successful ones. They sleep at the wrong time, eat at the wrong time, play music at the wrong time— I remember life was very difficult when we were all at home."

"And now?" Dirk's question was abrupt, as if he sensed the stress beneath her words.

"Now we all live our separate lives, in separate houses."

Holly tried not to remember the nursery with painted animals climbing the walls and aeroplane mobiles circumnavigating the ceiling.

She had locked the door when Martin died and never opened it again. His Lego was still in an untidy pile on the carpet, his toy cars parked on a plastic road beside the wardrobe. Eleanor had tried to make her clean it up, give the toys to Oxfam, but she had resisted from the start, knowing that the sight of his belongings, the fluffy animals on his bed, his battered books, would snap her tenuous hold on sanity. Then, later, when she began to reshape her life, she had got in the habit of ignoring the room, pretending that it wasn't there.

"You've never married?" Dirk sounded curious, as if he sensed a mystery behind her stilted reply.

"I was married," Holly answered abruptly. "My husband died."

She barely heard his murmured condolence.

Darren and his infidelities, his drunken abuse, and the stupid, careless overdose of drugs that had stunned a generation of teenagers. Darren had become a celebrity, with all the charisma and style that it entailed, so the rapidly expanding silhouette of her pregnancy was an embarrassment to him, something to be hidden from his fans, even denied for the sake of his public image. They had already separated by the time a mixture of drugs and alcohol claimed him, so Martin's birth a month later had been a chance to build a fresh start for herself.

Anxious to protect her small son from the publicity ensuing from his father's death, she had reassumed her maiden name and withdrawn from the frenetic music scene, rebuilding instead her own career in journalism and refusing all male overtures as she hurried home to Martin every evening, eager to claim him from his nanny. Gladly, after the disenchantment and pain of her marriage, she had given her son all her love.

"It all happened such a long time ago." Holly dismissed her memories with a strained smile. "I was very young," she added defensively, remembering suddenly that almost as much time had elapsed since Isabella Van Allen's death and, despite his lady-killer reputation, she was sure Dirk didn't view his loss so dismissively.

She glanced at him, her flirtatious air forgotten for a moment as the past besieged her. He was motionless, his eyes sombre. She must do something, anything, to stop him remembering his own tragedy.

"I'd love a brandy," she murmured, wincing inwardly at her own pushiness, even as she narrowed her eyes and tilted her head alluringly so that he could follow the long line of her throat.

"My pleasure." His introspective mood was broken as the shadows banished from his face, leaving it full of cool appraisal as his eyes fastened on her lips. She had deliberately moistened them with the tip of her tongue and his gaze travelled across her face with slow deliberation, lingering on the invitation of her parted lips and then climbing upwards until their gaze locked.

Scanned by his cool eyes, Holly's heart began to thud heavily against her ribs. She was a fool. Dirk Van Allen was already way ahead of her, laughing at her naivety. He knew that she was playing some sort of game and he was waiting, intrigued by her motives, sure of the attraction he held for her.

Momentary anger sparked in her eyes and he acknowledged it with a slight smile as he pushed back his chair. "Let us retire to the sitting-room and enjoy our brandy in comfort?" he suggested.

Holly allowed him to pull out her chair and then preceded him from the room without a word. The flush had faded from her cheeks, leaving them unnaturally pale. She could hardly blame Dirk for his present attitude. She had deliberately set out to captivate him, so it hardly mattered whether he recognised her flirtatiousness as a game or thought she was genuinely attracted to him. With his good looks, he was probably the recipient of many more serious advances, so she should feel glad that he wasn't annoyed by her obvious manoeuvring. Nevertheless, she felt a prickle of unease as they reached the sitting-room. She turned abruptly, intending to dispel the tension between them with a light remark.

He was immediately behind her, so her sudden halt brought them face to face, dangerously close in the dimly-lit corridor. Dirk's breath felt warm on her cheek. Words forgotten, she reached blindly for the door handle as she fought to control a sudden feeling of panic.

Dirk was faster, however, and their fingers tangled as they both tried to twist the handle. The hard pressure of his hand reawakened all the long-suppressed memories of Darren's drunken fumbling towards the end of their marriage. She swayed, her breath rasping in her throat, dizziness encroaching, until Dirk pushed the door open and switched on the overhead light, banishing the shadows.

"Is something wrong?" He stared down at her, noting her sudden pallor.

She pulled herself together with an effort. "I'm fine, just a little tired. Peter marched me miles around the zoological museum this afternoon."

He laughed and allowed himself to be distracted. "A brandy, I think you ordered," he said, waving her towards the sofa.

"Thank you." Holly tried to smile but her lips were stiff and traitorous and refused to comply. Deliberately she crossed the room and sat in a solitary armchair. She was beginning to realise the danger of the role she had chosen. Dirk was too experienced, too virile, to be satisfied with a mild flirtation. He would set the rules to any game he chose to play, and her reaction to his touch had shown her how badly she was equipped to cope; how, after all this time, Darren was still a dark shadow on her memory, sullying even casual physical contact. All she was fit for was deception and pretence, something her marriage had taught her only too well.

She closed her eyes tightly, willing the sudden scalding rush of tears not to fall, the surge of self-disgust a tangible lump in her throat. When she looked up, Dirk was standing over her, a brandy glass in either hand.

She took one, carefully avoiding his fingers, and raised it to her lips. It was very good brandy and it slipped down like liquid fire.

He hesitated for a moment and then, with a slight shrug, moved away, putting the width of the room between them as he chose a chair beneath his wife's portrait. Finally, as Isabella's lovely face came into focus, Holly realised the depths of her foolishness. She would never win the dangerous game she had started; Dirk would just use her, as he had used so many other women, to blur the pain of his loss. He was still possessed by the laughing face above the fireplace, and Peter's miniature resemblance to his mother made it impossible for him to let it go.

Chapter Three

Holly woke early the next morning with a shiver of apprehension. How could she go to Gorky Park with Dirk and Peter and continue with her silly flirtation? Last night had shown her only too clearly that she was out of her depth, that she couldn't play the game through to the outcome that Dirk expected. And to titillate him yet at the same time attempt to hold him at arm's length might do more harm than good, giving him even more reason to avoid Peter.

She pushed back the bedcovers and reached for her dressing-gown, too restless to remain in bed. It was still dark but she didn't bother to turn on the light. Instead, she pulled back the curtains and stared out. The curve of the Moscow River snaked beneath the shadow of the Kremlin. Farther off, high-rise concrete buildings soared towards the leaden sky. So much to see in such a short time. She mustn't waste the opportunity to start her book. For too long she had talked about it, hoping that its birth pangs would fill the emptiness of her life, but afraid to start in case, after all, it wasn't enough. Well, now she had more than enough to cope with. Peter, Dirk, Mrs. Malpass' suspicions, the research for her book... For the time being, at least, life wouldn't be empty. It was more than likely to overwhelm her with its multiplicity of emotions and moods.

She clenched her hands and turned away from the window. To blazes with it! Dirk Van Allen was still a rotten father and she was going to make him into a better one. She would just have to move more carefully, be less blatant in her approach so that he remained in doubt about her intentions. Surely that wasn't beyond her.

She was still deciding on the right behaviour for their trip to Gorky Park when Peter, too excited to sleep, burst into her bedroom. He was fully dressed, and he bounced on to her bed like any normal five-year-old.

"It's going to be a fine day. We are going skating, aren't we?"

"One thing at a time," she protested. "And you should knock before rushing into my bedroom."

"Sorry." Instantly he was subdued.

"Hey, it wasn't such a terrible crime." Holly tousled his hair. "How do you know it's going to be a fine day, anyway? Did Jack Frost inform you personally?"

His smile returned as he responded to her teasing. "Malpy says that if you can see the Lenin Hills, it will be a fine day."

"In that case, I'd better get dressed." She opened her wardrobe. "You go and play quietly in your room until I'm ready, and then we'll see about breakfast."

"Can't I stay here?" His face dropped. "I won't look while you get dressed," he offered generously. "You're not very interesting anyway. My last nanny was, though. She was fat and pink all over, like a pig. I used to peep through the keyhole."

"Peter!" Holly interrupted him before he disclosed anything further, and he grinned wickedly as he ensconced himself on the window-seat, a dimple shadowing his cheek.

"She wore a rubber thing, like a sausage skin," he added, determined to have the last word. "Her face went all red when she climbed into it."

* * *

Trying to control her laughter, Holly hurried through to the bathroom, her mind full of awesome imaginings. No wonder his last nanny had left, poor woman. He'd probably regaled everyone with a detailed description of her anatomy.

She splashed cold water on to her face, and shivered suddenly. What would he have in store for her if she didn't come up to scratch? Sobered by the thought, she returned to the bedroom and pulled on a thick red sweater over tights and woollen slacks. Topping the ensemble with a matching sleeveless cardigan, she turned to the mirror. Her face was too pale, the shadows under her eyes denoting more than an occasional sleepless night. Hastily, she used powder and lipstick to good effect, and then brushed her hair with an energy that made it curl and wave to her shoulders.

True to his word, Peter kept his eyes firmly on the window, not even moving while Holly bustled about the room, tidying her nightclothes and smoothing the crumpled bed. Nor did he complain when she attacked his own hair with her hairbrush. He waited patiently until she had finished, and then seized her hand.

"Come on," he said, opening the door. "Malpy is making pancakes for breakfast because she found some real maple syrup the last time we went to G.U.M." He mentioned Russia's biggest department store with easy familiarity.

Holly smiled at his worldliness and followed him obediently to the kitchen, trying to suppress her sudden apprehension about meeting Dirk again. She needn't have worried, however; Mrs. Malpass had laid only two places at table.

Holly's greeting was warm with relief. "Peter tells me that your pancakes are something special!"

"If the number he ate last time I made them is any indication, then they must be," the housekeeper answered drily, flipping a fresh pancake on to Peter's plate.

"He told me that you took him to G.U.M. to buy some maple syrup." Holly repeated Peter's words, hoping to produce a smile.

"Well, somebody has to look after the poor little soul." Mrs. Malpass gave her a sharp glance. "And his last nanny wasn't up to it."

Her manner implied doubts about Holly's ability too, and she realised that her behaviour the previous evening really had killed their blossoming friendship. She was sorry but bowed to the inevitable. There was too much at stake to worry about the housekeeper's opinion of her so, recognising that any further overtures were useless, she relapsed into silence. When Dirk entered the kitchen ten minutes later, he noticed the cool atmosphere immediately.

"I thought this was meant to be a treat!" he said, raising his eyebrows. "Why so glum?"

"I think we're still a bit sleepy." Holly blushed slightly as she took in his appearance. He was dressed casually but the Guernsey sweater and thick blue cords only added to his attractions. If Darren's shadow didn't stand between them, then flirting would be easy—Dirk was almost sinfully handsome.

"The fresh air will soon cure any sleepiness." He included them all in his smile. "That, together with a few falls on the ice, should have you wide awake in no time."

"I think I'll just watch you and Peter." Holly tried to excuse herself from full participation in the expedition. "As I can't skate at all, I'll only spoil things for you. And, besides, I haven't any skates."

"Oh no you don't. You're not going to wriggle out of something that was entirely your idea." Dirk's answering remark darkened the frown on Mrs. Malpass' face as her suspicions of Holly became more concrete. "We'll take you to G.U.M. and buy some skates, won't we, Peter?"

The little boy's face flushed pink with pleasure at his sudden inclusion in the conversation and he nodded eagerly, momentarily lost for words.

"That's settled then." Dirk poured himself some coffee and downed it in two mouthfuls. "Be ready in five minutes, both of you, because if we have to go via G.U.M. we had better leave early."

"Do you still want lunch at three, sir?" Mrs. Malpass didn't look at Holly.

"No, I don't think so. Miss Williams is in Moscow to do some research, as well as to look after Peter, so I think we'll introduce her to some authentic Russian food. In fact, you may as well take the day off. I'm sure we can fend for ourselves this evening."

"Thank you, sir." Mrs. Malpass looked anything but pleased as she turned away, her worst suspicions confirmed. Peter broke the sudden silence.

"Are we really going to eat out?"

"Didn't I just say so?' Dirk's answer was cool, slightly impatient, but Peter wasn't deterred. He was determined to make the most of the unexpected outing with his father.

"Can we go to the Russian Hut?" he pleaded. "Grandfather says we should go while we're in Moscow. He said it serves the best food in the whole of Russia."

"He's probably right," Dirk answered him automatically while his bold eyes shamelessly scrutinised Holly. She tried to distract him by saying she had read about the Russian Hut in her guide book.

"Surely it's a long way from central Moscow?"

"About an hour's drive," Dirk agreed, so too far to travel today." His eyes fixed blatantly on her mouth. "Perhaps you would like to go there one night instead Miss Williams?"

"Her name is Holly." Peter was kneeling in his chair, straining upwards so that he could see Dirk's face, anxious to participate in the conversation.

"Is it really?" A faint smile curved Dirk's mouth. "What a prickly name for someone so—delectable."

Only Holly heard the murmured reply as he left the kitchen, and she hid her face behind her coffee cup, waiting for the answering flush to fade. Dirk had left her in no doubt about his intentions. He was determined to pursue the promise of her flirtation and, in view of the proposed plans for the day, she didn't see what she could do about it.

* * *

Holly and Peter were only a few minutes later than their allotted five minutes, delayed by a search for Peter's boots until Holly remembered that he had kicked them out of sight beneath the hall-stand on the previous day. Dirk leaned against the door and watched his son scrabbling to retrieve them.

"That will teach you to put them away properly," he remarked with a good-natured grin. "You've just lost us three minutes of good skating time!"

Peter stared up at him, his hat askew over one eye, unable to believe that, far from being angry, his father was teasing him.

Holly helped him into his boots with a sigh of relief. Perhaps the outing wouldn't be too bad after all, not if she encouraged Dirk and Peter to skate together. They would, after all, be in crowds for most of the day, not exactly the ideal conditions for seduction, and she would plead tiredness when they returned to the apartment. She straightened Peter's hat and then followed Dirk down the stairs to the street, determined that today wouldn't fluster her.

It didn't take them long to reach G.U.M. and Dirk led them swiftly through the vast emporium, past alcoves offering everything from china and glassware to cotton and pins, without slackening his pace. By the time they arrived at an arcade selling sports equipment, they were hot and out of breath.

A sharp burst of Russian sent an assistant hurrying to a pile of boxes stacked on shelves behind a display of ski clothes, and soon they were surrounded by a selection of skates in various designs and colours.

47

"Try those on." Dirk pointed to a pair and then leaned against the wall, watching Holly struggle with her outdoor boots.

She pulled off her gloves and reached for the skates, her stockinged feet slipping easily into the soft leather. The assistant had chosen the right size and she began to tighten the laces, pulling the boots close round Holly's ankles.

"Are they comfortable?" Dirk was already peeling off a wad of bank notes and, when she nodded, he dropped them onto the counter.

She flushed as she pulled on her outdoor boots. "You must let me buy my own skates. I can't possibly allow you to pay for them."

"Too late." He pocketed the receipt with a nod of thanks to the smiling assistant and led the way to the nearest exit, not giving her a chance for further protest. And when they reached the street he didn't slow down but kept striding ahead, his own skates dangling from his shoulder. Holly and Peter had to run to keep up with him.

Eventually, despite their best efforts, they began to lag. Irritated by his impatience, as well as feeling hot and breathless, Holly stopped. He could hurry as much as he liked; she was not going to scuttle across Red Square like a bolting rabbit on her first visit. She would savour it; take her time. He would just have to wait.

She glanced across at Lenin's Mausoleum but the sombre structure, a massive truncated pyramid of red granite blocks, didn't attract her. Instead, her attention was taken by the cathedral, a fantastic fairy-tale building whose domes and spirals were painted in eye-catching rainbow colours.

"Whatever is that?" She clutched at Peter's arm.

"I don't know." He shrugged her off impatiently, anxious to catch up with his father. "It's just an old church."

"It's absolutely incredible." Holly stared at it in amazement. "I've never seen anything like it before."

48

"Nor are you likely to again." Dirk, finding himself alone, had retraced his steps and he grinned down at her, his face rosy from the cold air. "Ivan the Terrible had the architect blinded so he could never duplicate it."

"How appalling."

"Napoleon wouldn't have agreed. I think he wished that Ivan had done the deed before the cathedral was ever built. He called it a monstrosity and wanted to destroy it. He even allowed his soldiers to use it as a stable for their horses. It's worth a visit at night though," he added. "When it's illuminated, the independence of the Russian spirit really leaps out at you. Moscow has made it a national shrine, as a way of tying the past to the present."

Holly was fascinated, both by the outlandish architecture and by Dirk's apparent insight into modern Russia. She began to answer him, and then realised that Peter was no longer with them.

Dirk noticed her anxiety. "Peter is visiting the Place of the Skull, one of his favourite haunts when he comes to Red Square."

"It sounds horrible." Holly gave a shudder as they turned away from the cathedral.

"It doesn't look much now," Dirk explained as they caught up with Peter and stared at an unadorned round platform built of white stone, "but in medieval times hundreds of people were put to death here." He waved a hand in the direction of the cathedral. "Ivan used to choose the daily torture after his morning prayers."

"They don't do it any more, though." Peter dismissed the subject and skipped ahead, suddenly bored with the past.

"They don't need to." Dirk's eyes lost their relaxed humour as he turned away from the platform, and his voice was so low that Holly wondered if he was talking to her or merely thinking aloud. "Nowadays we can choose our own torture, and sometimes it lasts a lifetime."

She followed him silently, watching him wrestle with his change of mood. Neither of them spoke as they followed Peter out of the square and down a narrow road parallel with the river. A dark-coloured car, painted with the distinctive chequered band of a taxi, drove slowly past. Dirk flagged it down with a peremptory wave.

"Gorky Park." His instruction was curt, almost rude, but the driver didn't appear to notice. He merely waited for them to close the door and then took a sharp turn towards the outer ring of the city.

Peter, squeezed between Dirk and Holly, peered wide-eyed out of the window. He didn't speak, however, and the journey passed in complete silence until the moment the driver deposited them at the gigantic stone porch that marked the main entrance to the park.

"Please hurry." Peter, finding his tongue at last, pulled at Holly's sleeve. "Look, lots of people are already skating." He pointed to a crowd of people, warmly wrapped in coats and scarves, who were skating in time to the music blaring from the loudspeakers that lined the pathways.

Holly sank on to a wooden bench with a sigh of relief. She was already cold, and was also finding Dirk's sudden change of mood a strain.

"You both go on," she urged as they fastened their skates. "Let me watch for a while so I can see what I'm letting myself in for."

"Ten minutes, that's all you have." A glimmer of humour returned to Dirk's eyes. "After that you're skating, right, Peter?"

"Right." Peter carried on lacing up his own boots but his face flushed with pride as spoke to him like an equal.

* * *

Holly saw how their peculiar lurching gait as they crossed the snow-covered grass turned to a smooth glide as

50

soon as they stepped onto the ice. Other skaters whirled past her, their faces flushed and full of laughter. Even tiny children, younger than Peter, seemed full of confidence. It looked so easy that she decided perhaps she was worrying unnecessarily, and yet she still hesitated because she didn't want to make a fool of herself in front of Dirk.

"You haven't even put your boots on yet." He accused as he rejoined her. "Peter is already on his second circuit and he's sent me to fetch you."

Holly tried to hurry but she found the boots difficult to fasten under Dirk's amused gaze. Her fingers grew colder as she fumbled with the laces.

"Here, let me," he knelt beside her. "They're not the easiest things in the world to fasten."

"I've nearly finished." She bent further over her skates as she felt panic begin to build. The last thing she needed was for Dirk to touch her again.

"Don't be silly." He moved her hands firmly away from the boots and lifted her leg onto his knee. "There's a knack to winding the laces round the eyelets, and unless you do it tight enough you end up skating on your ankles." His fingers were warm and deft and he didn't look at her as he worked. When he finished the first one he lowered her foot to the ground and lifted the other one onto his bent knee. It was still clad in its warm, fur-lined boot which he tugged off, exposing her toes to the cold air.

"If you don't hurry Father, Holly's foot will freeze." shouted Peter who, impatient at their delay, had just jumped off the ice to join them. For answer, Dirk circled her toes in his warm hand and rubbed them gently.

Holly stiffened. She waited for the memories of Darren's brutality to take over, gritting her teeth against the expected dizziness, but instead an unfamiliar sensation of warmth swept over her. Instantly she tried to snatch her foot away, forgetting the encouragement she had given Dirk the previous evening, but he merely tightened his fingers and looked up with a grin.

51

"Disturbs you, does it?"

"No, it doesn't. I'm just ticklish." She blushed furiously, angry with him, and angry at herself for being so obvious. It was a great relief when the boot was finally fastened.

Dirk was still grinning as she stood up. "Do you want a hand?"

"No, thank you. I can manage perfectly well." She took a tentative step away from the bench, anxious to avoid his outstretched arm. The boots gripped her ankles like giant hands, displacing her weight, unbalancing her, and she stumbled.

"You ought to help her." Peter looked anxious.

"No, I can do it." Holly gestured him away indignantly but the sudden movement proved to be her undoing. Flat on her back, she glared up at Dirk who was laughing openly.

"I think this is one occasion when pride has to take a back seat," he chuckled, as he hauled her to her feet. "Peter will be disappointed if you don't skate, and if you can't even walk on firm ground on your own then you certainly won't be able to manage the ice."

Holly gave up. The vast frozen pond filled her with alarm and she knew he was right. She held out a reluctant hand.

Peter grabbed it, unable to understand her fear. "It's easy, really it is. Let me show you."

"Don't Peter!" Holly's voice rose to a shriek of alarm as he threatened to unbalance her again. "Let your father help me. He's stronger," she added weakly as Dirk slipped an arm round her waist.

"An invitation and a compliment," he teased her. "It must be my lucky day."

Holly didn't answer as she moved stiffly beside him, concentrating on remaining upright, anything to avoid closer contact. But as they stepped onto the ice, her legs shot from under her. Forgetting her intention of keeping Dirk at arm's length, she clutched at his coat in alarm.

"Just relax." He dropped his bantering tone and held her tightly. "It will take you a while to get your balance, so put your arm around me. That's better, now we're doubly secure."

His hand was warm across her back, firm at her waist. She concentrated on his instructions, willing herself to ignore his hands, willing herself to forget her unexpected reaction to the touch of his fingers on her foot.

"You're skating! You're really skating!" Peter darted round their rather jerky progress in excitement, his cheeks as red as his bright woollen scarf. "Can't you let go now, Father? Let's see if she can do it on her own now."

Dirk looked down at Holly with a grin as he slightly relaxed his hold.

"Don't!" She clutched at his coat, her sudden panic-stricken movement swinging her round to face him.

He tightened his grasp and grinned over her shoulder at Peter. "You can see my problem, can't you? Perhaps you'd better skate off on your own so as not to waste the morning."

"All right." Peter darted off to where several small boys were playing tag.

"He's too young to be alone." Unsuccessfully, Holly tried to move away from Dirk, her skates skidding awkwardly on the ice. This wasn't what she had planned at all. Dirk should be skating with Peter.

"Nonsense. He's perfectly safe. And, besides, I don't want him to see how much I envy him his nanny."

Holly, startled by such an open declaration, stopped worrying about whether she could stand upright and started worrying about something far more dangerous.

"Don't look so surprised," he told her. "I'm only following up last night's invitation."

"I don't know what you're talking about."

"Oh, yes, you do." He tucked an escaping curl back into her hat before letting his fingers trail down her cheek, coming to rest on the straight line of her mouth.

53

"Ah, don't, Holly." He rubbed his thumb gently across her lips. "Such a pretty mouth to look so stern."

Holly forgot that they were still on the ice and turned away, her cheeks scarlet with mortification. She was right out of her depth and it was her own fault. She had behaved stupidly.

She ceased her regrets as a passing skater jogged her, sending her legs in wildly opposite directions. Instinctively she grabbed at Dirk, allowing him to pull her close again.

"See, you can't resist me." He settled his arm round her waist, laughing at her gasp of indignation. "But as Peter is about to join us again, you'll just have to wait." He propelled her into the mainstream of skaters, giving her no time to protest.

Chapter Four

They skated for a long time until Holly's legs ached and her face was pink with effort. Even Peter seemed to be flagging, and finally she begged Dirk to stop.

"I don't think I can manage another step," she gasped. "My feet feel like lead."

He looked concerned, the teasing expression that had been there all morning fading from his eyes. "I'm sorry. I should have realised you'd get tired. Skating uses different leg muscles from walking."

He propelled her between groups of laughing skaters and swung towards the bank, half-lifting her onto the snow, his arms still tight around her waist. For a moment she felt the full length of his body against hers, warm and protective, and then she was alone, the bench hard under her aching legs.

Dirk loosened his skates and changed them for warm boots, tucking his blue cord trousers into the fur lining so that his legs seemed longer than ever. Peter, perched beside her on the bench, was chattering about the game he had played with a group of boys, and she nodded absently as she tugged at her laces, trying to dispel a sudden feeling of depression.

"Having trouble?" Dirk had pulled off Peter's boots and was now offering to do the same for her. She hesitated, knowing that her hands were too numb to do more than fumble with the laces but unwilling to submit further to his ministrations. Dirk, however, didn't wait for an answer as he tugged at her boots with firm hands.

She wiggled her toes in relief as he freed them, but a moment later she was gasping with pain as cramp locked them into position.

"Press down on to my hand," he ordered, pulling off his wet leather glove and pushing his palm against her toes. "Go on, harder. It will soon go. It's a combination of the cold and all those overworked muscles."

"I'm all right now." Holly winced as the circulation began to flow through her foot, filling it with pins and needles.

"Let me carry on rubbing your toes for a little longer." Dirk frowned as she slipped her feet into her boots. "It will take a moment for the blood to start circulating properly."

"No!" Holly's refusal was sharper than she intended because Dirk's palm, warm against her foot, his other hand massaging her instep, had produced the same tiny shivers of sensation she had felt earlier, reminding her that her long-denied body had not, after all, been rendered entirely unresponsive by Darren's infidelities and cruelty. She turned away, confused by the sudden conflict of her emotions.

"I think I prefer you on the ice," Dirk teased her, aware of her discomfort. "You're far too prickly once you're on firm ground. Perhaps your parents named you wisely after all."

Holly glared back at him, frightened by the strange reaction of her body and angry that he had noticed it and deliberately stroked her foot seductively while she was helpless. He was insufferable, and so ready to believe that all women would find him attractive that it was almost laughable. She wouldn't feel sorry for him a moment longer. If he wanted to dull the memory of his own loss with meaningless and well-publicised affairs, then he could count her out. She had been crazy even to think that she could fake a flirtation. Peter would just have to take his chances. Perhaps today had given him a start.

She thrust her hands in her pockets and turned into the wind, ignoring Dirk's chuckle of triumph as she started to trudge towards the exit.

"I think you forgot something." He caught up with her, her skates dangling from his hand.

"Thank you." Holly reached for them, her voice stiff and unforgiving, but instead of the hard steel of the blades she found her hand engulfed in Dirk's as he swung her skates over his shoulder.

"Stop sulking," he commanded, his eyes belying his stern expression. "You're setting Peter a bad example."

"He's not watching." Holly glanced across to where Peter was endeavouring to chip some splinters from a mound of dirty ice, and tried to pull her hand free.

"Nevertheless, as your employer, I insist that you smile." Dirk tightened his fingers and pulled her closer.

"Stop it, you're hurting me." Holly tried to wriggle out of his grasp, the memory of her recent response to him too close. With a sob of desperation in her voice, she pleaded with him. "Please, Mr. Van Allen, let me go."

His eyes narrowed. "Why so formal? After everything that has happened this morning the least you could do is to call me Dirk."

"All right, please let me go, Dirk." Holly spat the words out, suddenly very angry. Until now she had made allowances, guiltily aware that her own behaviour had roused his interest, and anxious to withdraw gracefully without the trauma of a confrontation that might upset Peter. But there were limits to her patience and she didn't intend that Dirk Van Allen should act as if he owned her.

"Why?" His fingers were still tight around her hand. "Last night I could have sworn that this was exactly what you had in mind."

"That was last night." Holly stopped struggling as angry tears spilled on to her cheeks.

"And now you've changed your mind." He pulled her closer, his voice silky and threatening. "I don't like cheats,

Holly—girls who offer more than they're prepared to give."

"And I don't like arrogant, self-opinionated men who expect every woman to fall swooning at their feet," Holly snapped, jerking angrily at her arm. She knew she owed Dirk an apology for her earlier behaviour but she was damned if she was going to give him one. He moved too fast, expected too much from a casual flirtation. He could rot in his own misery as far as she was concerned. Anxiously, she looked round for Peter, hoping to defuse the situation. He came running over, grinning widely when she called him.

"Are we going to eat now?" he asked.

"Of course." Dirk released Holly's hand, his voice normal despite the stormy expression in his eyes. "I booked a table at the Aragvi for three o'clock. In fact, we'd better find a taxi quickly or we'll be late."

"I can see one." Peter ran ahead to the park entrance and waved in vain to a passing Moskvich car. When it didn't stop he ran further down the pavement, leaving Holly and Dirk alone.

* * *

They stared at one another in silence. "It seems that we both made a mistake," Dirk said finally.

Holly nodded uncomfortably. "I'll return to England as soon as you find a replacement," she offered, thinking that it would be impossible for them to remain in the same house without embarrassment.

"I hardly think that's necessary." He was cool and formal as he guided her towards the entrance. "After all, we both have a responsibility towards Peter and, as he obviously likes you far more than any of his previous nannies, he would be sorry to see you go. Surely we can behave like civilised people and forget the past twenty-four hours? I'm rarely at home anyway, so I don't think you'll find life too difficult at the apartment; that is, if you can

58

survive the few hours between now and Peter's bedtime?" Surprisingly, he gave a wry smile.

She nodded reluctantly. Angry though she was, she accepted her own part in the misunderstanding, agreed too that it would be churlish to leave if Dirk wanted her to stay. Peter had already experienced enough disturbance in his short life without a disagreement between his father and his nanny disrupting it further.

"In that case, let's call a truce." Dirk offered her his hand. "Here's to our new business relationship."

Holly touched his fingers briefly with a tremulous hand, and he laughed. "I keep my word, you know. No more unwelcome passes. Just one word of advice, though. Other men might react differently, so be careful, Holly. You are a very attractive woman and there are several unattached men at the Embassy."

"Don't worry," Holly answered him with some of her old spirit. "I rarely make the same mistake twice."

"In this instance, I think I'm entitled to feel a little disappointed." He smiled down at her, his attempt at humour drawing the sting from his remark. Despite herself, Holly gave an answering smile.

"That's better." He waved to a cruising taxi and called to Peter. "Now I'm going to take you to one of Moscow's most popular restaurants and let you experience real Russian cuisine."

* * *

They arrived at the Aragvi shortly after three and were quickly ushered through to a large dining area decorated with rich murals. An attractive waitress with lustrous dark eyes smiled up at Dirk, her admiration for his striking appearance obvious. Holly sighed. No wonder he was so arrogant and self-assured.

She managed a smile of thanks as they were shown to a table beneath a low, richly painted archway, and then she concentrated on Peter, removing his coat and hat and draping them over the back of his chair.

"Shall I order or would you like to try?" Dirk picked up the menu. "Chicken *Zatsivi* is their speciality, but it's a cold dish, so perhaps not entirely suitable after a morning's skating."

"Please, you choose." Holly shrugged herself out of her cardigan. "I know so very little about Russian food that I'm prepared to try anything."

"You too, Peter?" Dirk asked his son.

"I want a *sulguni*." Peter was showing off for Holly's benefit.

"Please," she reacted automatically.

"Please," he repeated obediently, a little downcast by her response. Dirk gave a faint smile and then addressed the waitress in Russian before turning back to Peter and Holly.

"I've ordered three *sulguni* as appetisers, and two chicken *tabaka* to follow, with an extra plate for Peter for the main course."

"That's not fair." Peter reacted like any typical five-year-old, his voice rising in indignation. "I want a chicken *tabaka* of my own."

Holly interrupted Dirk's sharp retort hastily. "And then who would help me with my meal? I can't possibly eat that much on my own."

He subsided, slightly mollified, and Dirk's frown faded as he leaned back in his chair, although he still looked faintly irritated.

Anxious to distract him from Peter, Holly asked about the food he'd ordered. He raised a quizzical eyebrow as he answered, recognising her ploy but prepared to respond.

"All the dishes served here originate from Georgia," he explained. "That's a small mountainous region on the Black Sea that remained independent for many years and, consequently, has a very different culture from central Russia."

60

The waitress returned with three plates and a basket of freshly baked bread. Dirk broke off from his explanation and smiled his 'I'll captivate you at any price' smile. The girl flushed a rosy pink and, with her eyes demurely lowered, flicked a glance at Holly to see if she'd noticed.

Holly simply looked through the waitress, her expression glacial, and Dirk chuckled.

"You can't have it both ways. If you are off limits then at least allow me a little pleasure elsewhere. Besides, the waitresses here are all so pretty that it's a shame not to appreciate them."

"Another import from Georgia, I suppose," Holly snapped, unaccountably annoyed by his mild flirtation.

"Careful," he warned, his grin growing wider, "your claws are showing!"

"What nonsense." Holly hastily changed her expression to a warm smile as the waitress returned with the *sulguni*. "You really do have the most fantastic ego, Mr. Van Allen."

"From you, that almost sounds like a compliment."

"Why do you call my father Mr. Van Allen?" Peter interrupted.

"Because he's my employer, Peter," Holly replied, biting back a more truthful remark. Peter seemed satisfied with her explanation but Dirk seized upon the subject with relish.

"It does sound a bit ridiculous, doesn't it? 'Mr. Van Allen while we're living under the same roof."

"It's what Mrs. Malpass calls you," Holly countered reasonably.

"Ah, but she doesn't come skating with us, does she, Peter?" Dirk gave a sardonic smile. "Shall we put it to the vote? Hands up if you think Holly should call me Dirk."

Peter's hand shot up instantly, enjoying the game, and Dirk nodded, satisfied.

"Two to one Holly. You've lost, I'm afraid."

"Then I must bow to the majority." She tried to smile for Peter's sake but she was upset by Dirk's ploy. Despite his apparently graceful acceptance of her changed behaviour, he hadn't really forgiven her at all. She had dented his pride, allowed him to make a fool of himself, and he wasn't going to let her off lightly. Something told her that she was going to have to pay for her few hours of foolhardy flirtation.

* * *

She was proved right far too quickly. They were halfway through the crisp *sulguni*, a deep-fried cheese eaten with new bread, when Dirk was hailed from across the room. He acknowledged the greeting with a smile, and a pink-faced Russian, plump and bespectacled, hurried across to their table.

"*Zdrahst vwy tye*," he greeted Dirk in Russian, and they then held an unintelligible conversation for a few minutes while Holly sat, her fork poised, waiting patiently to finish her *sulguni*.

However, when Dirk turned to her with a smile and introduced her as '*moy preyahtyel*' she didn't need any knowledge of the language to understand the inflection in his voice, nor the sudden flicker of interest in the Russian's eyes. She smiled graciously, gritting her teeth as the pleasant little man apparently showered her with compliments. She continued to smile until he had bowed himself out of the restaurant. Then she glared at Dirk.

"That was a dirty trick."

"What did I do?" He was all innocence.

"You introduced me as...as...!" Holly spluttered, unable to utter the appropriate words.

"I merely told him you were my friend." Dirk sounded aggrieved as he turned to Peter for confirmation. "Isn't that right, Peter? Didn't I say that Holly was my friend?"

"Yes," Peter said through a mouthful of bread. "He said you were his *preyahtyel*. That means friend. You are, aren't you?" he asked anxiously. "And my friend too?"

"Of course I'm your friend." Holly ignored the first part of his question as she finished her *sulguni*. She was furious with Dirk but not sure how to handle him in Peter's presence, so she contented herself instead with a scowl. But Dirk's chuckle as the waitress cleared away their plates left her in no doubt that he was entirely unrepentant.

Although the rest of the meal was delicious, Holly's appetite was spoilt and she didn't do justice to the fried chicken *tabaka* which was served with a prune sauce and accompanied by pickled cabbage; and she refused a dessert, making Peter gasp with horror.

"You must have some ice cream," he insisted. "Grandfather says that Russia makes the best ice cream in the world!"

"As one of the world's ice cream connoisseurs, he's probably right." Dirk smiled at his son's enthusiasm. "I must admit that it's worth tasting; it's the real thing made from eggs, cream and sugar, with not a preservative in sight."

"And it's served with berry jam," Peter added.

"All right." Holly gave in gracefully, wondering at Peter's repeated references to his grandfather. Was it Dirk's father he was referring to, or the beautiful, Italian/Russian Isabella's? Before she could formulate the question, however, the ice cream arrived in a small silver dish, and she had to admit it was delicious.

"I told you," Peter crowed, digging into his with an enthusiasm that made both Holly and Dirk laugh.

"That's better," Dirk said softly. "You have a pretty laugh. I thought for a moment you weren't going to forgive me."

"I haven't yet," Holly snapped, still sore at his behaviour. "And you hadn't better try anything like that again or you'll be looking for another nanny."

He was still grinning. "You're too serious, Holly. You must learn to appreciate a joke. Last night you would have fluttered your eyelashes and played the part to perfection wouldn't you."

"Can we please forget last night? I've already said I'm sorry."

"Oh, but not properly." Dirk's hand shot across the table and he grasped her wrist, his fingers firm on a pulse that suddenly started throbbing as her heart beat faster.

"Well, in that case let me say it now," Holly gasped, trying to extricate her hand without alerting Peter to the tussle between them. Sudden tears of fright pricked her eyelids as she was reminded of another incident, during her marriage, when Darren had twisted her arm so badly that it had been bruised for weeks.

"Accepted." Surprisingly, Dirk released her and, without another word, turned to look for the waitress while a still oblivious Peter scraped his bowl with relish.

His change of mood was so abrupt, the alteration from scornful teasing to sombre withdrawal so swift, that Holly stared at him in surprise. He had gained the waitress' attention and ordered coffee, and now he was drawing patterns on the cloth with an unused fork, his brows drawn together in a frown.

"I really am sorry, you know." She forgot her own injured pride as she attempted to erase the bitterness from his face. Then, when he didn't answer her, she blurted out the first thing that came into her head.

"I made a bet with a friend. I said I could captivate you. You are very well-known in the gossip columns," she added defensively when he still didn't answer, wondering for one awful moment if she had only made matters worse.

"I must be if I'm fair game for bets." He gave a wry smile. "What will you tell your friend?"

"That I wasn't up to it." Holly laughed as she wondered what Eleanor would say if she ever learned of her attempt to 'seduce' Dirk Van Allen. "She would never believe anything else anyway. I'm not exactly a *femme fatale,* am I? After all you've had plenty of experience of those, haven't you?"

"Have I indeed?" Dirk threw down the fork and leaned back in his chair. "Remind me."

"Well, you escorted Deanna Robin to the premiere of her latest film, and you were seen on three separate occasions with Lisette du Près, the soprano; once in Paris, once in Rome and once in London."

When he remained silent, she mentioned several other names she remembered from Eleanor's newspaper clippings.

"You've done your homework well," he replied at last. "Should I be flattered that you've followed my romantic career so carefully, or is there a more mundane explanation?"

"I...the agency showed me the cuttings." Holly became flustered as she realised the implications of her admission to Eleanor's agency. But she needn't have worried; Dirk's burst of laughter was so spontaneous that it drew answering smiles from surrounding tables.

"Bravo for the English Nanny. No stone left unturned in the search for the truth. I'm surprised the agency sent you, though. Surely someone starchy and grey-haired would have been more suitable for an employer with my reputation."

"I was considered immune," Holly said primly.

"I think I've just been insulted. Never mind. We're well and truly quits now, Miss Holly Williams."

"Just call her Holly," Peter told his father, his ice cream finished and boredom setting in.

"Ah, but I haven't heard her call me Dirk yet." He gave a mock frown, good humour completely restored. "Perhaps we'd better stay formal after all."

"You're not to." Peter looked upset. "We voted on it, you know we did. Go on, shake hands and agree."

"One of your better ideas, Peter," Dirk replied, and seized Holly's hand.

"Hello, Holly."

"Hello, Dirk." She felt foolish as his fingers engulfed hers, and an unexpected warmth suffused her face.

"Nobody who can still blush should be fodder for the gossip columns," he murmured, continuing to hold her hand. "I promise to introduce you properly in future."

* * *

When they left the restaurant it was dark, and they had to walk for some minutes before a taxi would stop. Peter skipped along between them, his furry hat bobbing along at elbow height as he swung from Holly's hand. She noticed that he didn't attempt to hold on to Dirk, but she felt nevertheless that Dirk was reacting more naturally towards him, answering his questions and putting a restraining fatherly hand on his shoulder when they had to cross a road.

Despite the traumas of the day, she began to relax. Now they had cleared up their misunderstandings, perhaps she and Dirk could be friends of a sort; something she certainly hadn't contemplated when she first met him. Maybe simple friendship was, after all, the way to help him through his problems with Peter. With the boy's trust already half gained, she could act as a go-between, encouraging them both to make allowances for each other.

She gave a wry smile. Such a simple explanation—and to think that she had put herself through ridiculous torments trying to make herself alluring when all it needed was mutual respect and a little good will. She had reckoned without Mrs. Malpass though.

* * *

When they finally reached the apartment block, Dirk hurried them up the stairs.

"Come on, you two," he said, sounding almost jovial. "Let's get inside out of this infernal cold." He unlocked the

66

door and switched on the hall light, pulling off his hat as he did so, his blond hair tousled and boyish under the yellow glare of the light.

Peter kicked off his boots and then, at a warning glance from Holly, picked them up and carried them through to the kitchen. He was back in a moment, waving an envelope.

"Malpy's gone out. She left a letter."

"I expect it's to tell us that supper is in the oven." Dirk received it with a smile and opened it while hanging up his coat.

Holly moved towards the kitchen, intending to put her boots with Peter's. She had almost reached the door when a sharp exclamation from Dirk stopped her in her tracks.

"Is something the matter?" she asked.

"That's one way of putting it." He crumpled the letter savagely in his hand. "Your lamentable attempt to captivate me for the sake of a silly bet has just produced another nasty repercussion. Mrs. Malpass has gone off sick."

"I don't understand." The blood drained from Holly's face leaving two red spots of colour high on her cheekbones which showed that she did understand, only too well.

Dirk gave a scornful smile. "Don't try and play the innocent, Holly. I thought we had agreed to be honest with each other at least. It seems we have offended her sensibilities so she has succumbed to an unnamed virus until I come to my senses and throw you out."

"I don't believe she wrote that," Holly gasped in indignation.

"Not in so many words, no" he admitted, "but her sudden illness makes it transparently obvious. Mrs. Malpass is not usually given to impulse—even germs have to give her prior warning." His mouth twisted into a tight smile. "She is, however, a woman of irreproachable character and reliability, and consequently rather too easily shocked."

"I can't imagine why she agreed to work for you then," Holly snapped, irritated by his assumption that she was the only cause of his housekeeper's desertion. "It takes two to tango, you know. Besides, most employers would have a more robust reputation in the first place, one that would not be so easily jeopardised by an evening's mild flirtation."

"I suppose I deserve that." Dirk's anger faded and he looked rueful. "But it doesn't solve my problem does it? You are now stuck in an apartment with me, a fading reputation, and no chaperon; not exactly a situation calculated to send you back to the agency with a good reference."

"I expect I'll weather it," Holly said, mollified by his change of attitude. "After all, I don't intend to continue nannying, and writers rarely have a good reputation anyway."

"Then you'll stay and look after Peter despite the situation?"

"I hardly think I've much choice." It was Holly's turn to look rueful now. "After all, I'm the one responsible for the misunderstanding."

Peter had remained silent while they were talking, looking from one to the other with interest. Suddenly, he gave an excited jump.

"Is Holly going to look after everything while Malpy is away? Even cook?"

"Something like that." Dirk nodded absently.

"Then will she be like a mother?"

Holly heard the wistful note in his voice and a lump rose in her throat. "Not a mother, darling," she told him as she impulsively picked him up, holding him as she would have held Martin. "More like a very special friend. Can you cook?" she asked, trying to lighten the situation as she felt his arms tighten round her neck and noticed the disappointment in his eyes.

"I don't know. I've never tried."

"Well, perhaps we'd better find out," she said, giving him a quick hug. "How about starting with your bedtime drink?"

"You can add a cup of tea to that," Dirk said quickly.

"Don't you want to learn too?" Peter suddenly put out an arm and clasped Dirk round the neck. The unexpected movement pulled Holly off balance, making her sway forward so that the three of them were so closely grouped their heads almost touched. For a tiny fraction of a second Dirk reacted spontaneously, his eyes crinkling with laughter as he put his arms around them, hugging them both. Then, just as suddenly, he withdrew.

"I'll be in my study," he said as he abruptly turned away.

"Come along, Peter." Holly took the few steps to the kitchen where she lowered him onto a stool. "Now, the first thing you must remember before you start cooking is— always wash your hands." She pushed the stool towards the sink. She was trying to blot out Dirk's behaviour with a rush of words hoping Peter hadn't noticed his sudden coldness. It didn't work. Instead of turning on the tap, Peter squirmed round and threw his arms about her neck, burying his head in her shoulder.

"Why doesn't my daddy like me?" he sobbed.

Holly held him close, feeling his heart beating fast against hers. It was the first time she had heard him refer to Dirk as daddy and it made her want to cry. "Of course he likes you. It's only because he still misses your mother that he doesn't always show you how much. Sometimes he just feels too sad."

"It's because I killed her, isn't it?" Suddenly Peter looked much older, his face pinched and pale. "I killed her when I was born."

"What nonsense." Holly tried to hug him again but he pushed her away. "Your mother just died. It wasn't your fault. Of course your father doesn't blame you."

"He does." Peter turned away from her and filled the bowl with water. "He hates me." Then he shrugged, as if he was dismissing Dirk from his mind. "I don't care anyway. I was only pretending."

"Good." Holly's voice almost broke as she accepted his lie. How could she bear his unhappiness? How could Dirk do it to him? Angrily, she scrubbed at her hands and then seized the kettle and filled it at the sink.

"You make your bedtime drink and I'll make the tea. There might even be some biscuits if we look hard enough."

"They're in the blue tin." Peter's voice was matter-of-fact as he dried his hands, his emotions under tight rein. Holly knew that if she looked at him his eyes would have Dirk's shuttered look. She clenched her hands, remembering the brief moment in the hall when they had all seemed to belong together. She remembered Dirk's arm round her shoulders, his face so close. For a split second, he and Peter had filled the void in her life by providing the warmth and comfort she had denied herself for so long. It was ridiculous: a man she had only known for two days and a little boy with too many problems, and already her self-control was crumbling.

She didn't even like Dirk. He was too much of a lady-killer, too arrogant; all the things that her brief marriage to Darren had taught her to hate. And his treatment of Peter merely compounded her dislike. How dare he be so wrapped up in his own misery that he excluded his child?

* * *

She made the pot of tea and helped Peter mix his bedtime drink in a fury of determination. Then, making sure that he was comfortable at the kitchen table with a mug of malted milk and two biscuits, she carried Dirk's tea through to the study.

She would have it out with him; let him see how damaging his behaviour was. After all he could hardly

70

throw her out until he managed to contact Mrs. Malpass, so that gave her a few days to take advantage of their new relationship.

The door was open when she reached the study, and Dirk was talking on the telephone. She hesitated as she put his cup on the desk and when he motioned that she should stay, walked over to the window and stared across at the black shadows of the Kremlin. For a moment she drank in the scene, the silent thread of river, the quietness; then Dirk's conversation began to impinge. She stiffened slightly as he used an endearment. He was obviously talking to a girlfriend, arranging a meeting. The anger that she had been holding in check swelled into bitterness as she listened.

"I won't keep you for more than a few moments," he said, replacing the telephone receiver. "I just thought I'd clarify my arrangements for the next few days. I shall be out most of the time so you will have an almost completely free rein with Peter."

He took out his wallet and counted out a wad of notes. "This will keep you going for a few days. Tomorrow I'll ask Stephen Andrews to sort out a banking arrangement for you so that you don't run short of money because, until Mrs. Malpass returns, I'm afraid you will have to cope with the shopping as well."

Holly put out her hand automatically and accepted the money. It seemed far too much for her day-to-day needs. She began to speak but Dirk interrupted her, his tone cool and impersonal.

"I shall rarely be in for a meal, and the embassy takes care of my laundry." He stood up, draining his tea in one mouthful. "Have you any questions? No, then I'll be on my way." He took Holly's silence at face value. "I've arranged to meet a friend this evening and I'll probably return home very late."

Holly stared at him, dismayed by his sudden return to formality. Admittedly it was better than his attempted intimacy, but it was still unexpected; almost a slap in the face. What had happened to change him? Was it Peter and the moment they had shared in the hall, or was it something deeper? She frowned, deeply disappointed that in the face of his sudden unfriendliness she couldn't fight for Peter; couldn't even mention him.

"Thank you for the money," she said coolly. "Is there anything else, because if not I'd like to put Peter to bed."

Twenty minutes later, while she was reading Peter a bedtime story, Dirk put his head round the bedroom door.

"I've put a spare key on the kitchen table," he said.

"Thank you." Holly tried to ignore his appearance although from his silk shirt and tight-fitting trousers, it was quite apparent that his outing was unofficial.

"Say good night to your Father because he's going out," she instructed Peter.

Peter's "Good night" was barely audible.

Dirk didn't smile or attempt to approach the bed. Instead, he nodded curtly to both of them and left the room.

* * *

Shortly afterwards the front door slammed and Holly, noticing Peter's pinched expression, read him a second story, and then a third, until his eyelids began to droop. Gently she eased him down into the bed, tucking the covers tightly round him.

"Good night, darling," she whispered, bending towards him.

He didn't answer but immediately turned away, burrowing under the covers so that only the top of his head showed. Holly straightened up, feeling rebuffed. So much for opening herself up to the outside world. First Dirk and now Peter had rejected her, had shown her that they didn't want her friendship. Dirk was only interested in her as a conquest, an interest that had waned rapidly once she set the record straight, and Peter only wanted Dirk.

72

She closed the bedroom door quietly behind her and stared at herself in the hall mirror. 'I should never have let Eleanor persuade me. I seem to have moved from total isolation to total involvement—and they are both equally painful. In future you keep out of other people's affairs, Holly Williams,' she told her pale-faced reflection. 'Just concentrate on your book; that's what you came to Moscow for, remember?'

She gave a shaky laugh, dismayed by her own stupidity. After all, Darren and Martin had both rejected her, too, in their different ways. Why should she expect more from total strangers?

Chapter Five

She jumped as the doorbell rang. Perhaps Mrs. Malpass had had second thoughts and she could explain everything to her. Anything would be better than sitting alone trying to come to terms with her own stupidity. She hurried to the door and threw it open eagerly. Stephen Andrews was standing outside, smiling.

"I saw Mr. Van Allen go out as I left the Embassy so I decided to be neighbourly. I hoped you might like some company."

Holly gave him a warm smile, relieved that she no longer need be alone with her thoughts. "Please come in," she said, holding the door open.

He didn't need a second invitation. "How have the first two days been?" he asked her as he followed her through to the sitting-room

"Not too bad. Peter took me to the zoological museum yesterday, and we all went skating today."

"Mr. Van Allen as well?" Stephen's eyebrows shot up above his glasses.

"Yes." Holly laughed to see his surprise. "He skates very well."

"I'm sure he does. I mean, he's the sort of person who does everything well, isn't he? I don't suppose he's ever failed at anything in the whole of his life, do you?"

Hearing the note of envy in his voice, Holly frowned. "You sound as if you're speaking from the heart."

"I am. I mean—he's got everything; looks, money, talent. He'll leap into the post of American Ambassador in a few years' time, or some other plum job, while I plod my way through the lower echelons in my size nines." Stephen waggled his foot at Holly with a wry grin. "Mind you, he's a good boss; the best I've worked for. He gives me plenty of scope; believes in delegating and then trusting his staff to get on with it."

"Like meeting me at the airport," she teased.

"That was one of my better assignments." Stephen flashed her a glance that was warm with admiration. "Most of them fall into a different category. Our work is mainly statistics—looking at the growth and changes in Moscow during the last decade, and the way the city is developing today."

"Then Mr. Van Allen is not actually a diplomat?"

"Not yet," Stephen agreed. "Although I'm sure he will be soon because he already attends most of the functions. His father was a senior diplomat here a decade or so ago, and his wife was the daughter of an Italian ambassador who married a Russian countess. That's why he has this splendid apartment," he gestured around the richly furnished sitting-room. "It belongs to his wife's family and he uses it whenever he's in Moscow. I must say it's considerably better than my pokey two-roomed apartment in the back of beyond."

"Poor Stephen," Holly sympathised. "How about a coffee to cheer you up?"

"I thought you'd never ask." He followed her into the kitchen with all the brash confidence of youth, making her feel considerably older than the four or five years between them.

"This is nice too," he commented, looking round the well-equipped kitchen approvingly.

"It is, isn't it?" She answered absent-mindedly as she spooned coffee into two mugs, her thoughts still on their previous conversation. It explained Peter's frequent references to his grandfather as both sets of grandparents were obviously familiar with Moscow. It also explained the portrait of Isabella in the sitting-room, dispelling her earlier assumption that it travelled from country to country with

Dirk so that he could hang it in every rented sitting-room and feed his anguish into an unhealthy obsession. The portrait clearly belonged to his dead wife's family.

She poured boiling water from the kettle and offered Stephen sugar and milk before returning to the subject.

"What do you know about Mr. Van Allen's wife?"

"Only that she was a beautiful woman. According to some of the older members of the embassy staff, theirs was the grandest wedding of the year. When she died, just after Peter was born, nobody could quite believe it. Apparently, he never mentions her."

"And yet her death colours the rest of his life," Holly said, almost to herself. "His talent and wealth are dust and ashes compared to the loss of his wife."

"He seems to console himself pretty well," Stephen declared, too young and untouched by tragedy himself to see the effects of Isabella's death.

Holly noticed the tinge of bitterness in his voice with an inward smile. So that was the basis of his envy: Dirk's success with women. She stood up and changed the subject.

"Let's go back into the sitting-room; I think there are some records we can play."

* * *

Stephen stayed until eleven, and by the time he left, after a second cup of coffee, they had arranged to meet the following day.

"I'm free all of tomorrow," he told her. "Perhaps we could visit a few museums or something. Anything you like."

"And Peter too," Holly bargained, remembering his reaction when she told him she intended to immerse Peter in Russian culture.

"Peter, too," he agreed with a groan. "But don't forget the handcuffs."

"Don't be so mean," she protested. "He's been an angel today, and for most of yesterday, too, for that matter."

"He's just lulling you into a false sense of security." Stephen pulled on his coat. "Ten o'clock tomorrow?"

"Ten o'clock," she agreed, opening the door.

He smiled down at her, a question in his eyes.

She took a step backwards, her voice firm. "Good night, Stephen. Thank you for thinking of me."

"Difficult not to." He looked glum for a moment, recognising her brush off, knowing that he was not going to get a hoped for kiss. Then he laughed, acknowledging his chagrin with a joke.

"At least I'm one notch up on Mr. Van Allen. He must be slipping if he hasn't made a pass at you."

"I'm hardly in his league. Nor am I prepared to be a notch in anyone's belt, so don't get ideas Stephen."

He flushed with embarrassment, looking even younger than he really was. "I didn't mean to imply…"

"I know you didn't," she reassured him. "But it's only fair to let you know where you stand."

"Yes, of course." He looked so thoroughly miserable, like a red-faced small boy in trouble, that Holly relented and patted his arm.

"Don't look so woebegone," she told him. "I've already said that I'll be delighted to spend tomorrow with you. Now go home, and Peter and I will meet you at ten o'clock, handcuffs and all."

He bounded down the stairs two at a time, spirits totally restored, and Holly closed the door behind him.

She sighed as she began to tidy the sitting-room. She wasn't sure she ought to encourage Stephen at all, but his appearance, so soon after Dirk's inexplicable change of mood, had been the answer to a prayer. Besides, Moscow was a beautiful city and one that ought to be shared. And as Stephen obviously felt that acting as her escort would give him a little kudos amongst his contemporaries, they were, in a funny way, exchanging favours.

She returned a record to its dust cover and replaced it in the rack. Pausing for a moment, she met Isabella's eyes, dark and mysterious, as they stared across the room.

"You've a lot to answer for," she said aloud. "Just let him go. Let him find some sort of peace before he destroys your son."

"Do you make a habit of talking to yourself?" Dirk's voice set her spinning round in confusion.

"I…I didn't hear you come in." It was Holly's turn to blush as she wondered if he had heard her exact words.

"So I gather." He grinned wolfishly but the humour didn't reach his eyes.

Holly noticed his flushed cheeks with alarm and, as he came closer, she could smell Cognac, pungent and warm, on his breath.

"You've had a visitor." He slurred his words slightly as he spoke and she realised that he had drunk a very great deal of Cognac.

"Yes, Stephen came to see how I was settling in," she said, backing away.

"Nice of him." Dirk took another step towards her. "But just remember one thing, Holly: Stephen Andrews is very young. Don't play the sort of game with him that you tried on me."

"I don't intend to, not that it's any business of yours what I do, provided it doesn't affect Peter."

"It is my business when a member of my staff is involved," he said with a scowl. "Stephen is a very promising young man and I'll not have you distracting him from his work."

"Don't worry," she said from the safety of the doorway. "I assume your praise means that you think he's a promising Van Allen carbon copy, and as you already know, I wouldn't touch that with a barge pole."

She slammed the door behind her and ran along the corridor, expecting at any moment to hear Dirk behind her.

She reached her bedroom safely, however, and closed the door with a great sigh of relief. Thank goodness she had her own bathroom and didn't need to enter the main apartment again. Perhaps by the morning Dirk would be more himself, whatever that meant. She despaired of ever truly finding out. But one thing she did know: she was extremely thankful to have escaped so lightly from her ill-judged behaviour of the previous evening.

She hesitated a moment, then prudently turned the key in the lock. If drink was yet another of his problems, then she wasn't going to give him another chance to make a fool of himself. In future she would sleep behind a locked door.

* * *

Dirk didn't appear at breakfast the following morning, and Holly gave a sigh of relief as she and Peter left the apartment. Perhaps he would be out when they returned so she could avoid seeing him all day.

She glanced down at Peter, plodding along beside her with a glum look on his face. He had barely spoken since breakfast and had evinced no enthusiasm at all when she had told him about Stephen's proposed plans for the day.

"Cheer up," she said, holding out her hand for him to take. "You'll enjoy today's outing, Peter. We'll show you Ivan the Terrible's ivory throne."

He ignored her outstretched hand, the usual scowl darkening his face. "I'd rather go skating again," he told her, his voice stiff and unfriendly.

"Oh, come on." She tried to jolly him along, recognising, in his wish to re-live the previous day, his hopeless longing for his father. "You know you can't go skating every day."

"Why not?" He glared up at her, his eyes black and cold.

"Because I won't take you." Holly's patience was at an end. Peter had to learn some manners, regardless of his unhappiness. They marched on in silence, shoulders hunched against the cold, icy wind whistling round their heads, and by the time they reached Red Square, they were both thoroughly miserable.

* * *

Stephen, looking annoyingly cheerful and warm, was waiting for them beside the fantastic St. Basil's Cathedral.

"Hello, you two," he greeted them expansively. "Where do you want to start? Do you want to go into the cathedral or shall we tackle the Kremlin straight away?"

"The Kremlin, please." Holly smiled at him, suddenly very glad of his uncomplicated friendship. Peter, however, ignored him and ran across to the Place of the Skull.

Stephen raised his eyebrows. "Trouble?"

"I'm afraid so," Holly said with a sigh. "He's been so good since I arrived that I began to think your warnings were an exaggeration."

"The calm before the storm." Stephen dropped his arm across her shoulder in a sympathetic hug.

"Thank you very much. With friends like you, who needs enemies?" They were laughing together, Stephen's arm still around her shoulder, when Peter returned. His scowl deepened when Stephen began to tell him stories about Ivan the Terrible.

"I already know," he interrupted rudely. "My father told me. He knows everything about Moscow."

He marched past them towards the Spassky Gate, not sparing them another glance.

"Well and truly put in my place," Stephen murmured. "What a shame his father's talents don't stretch to instilling manners in small boys."

Holly was worried. "I do hope he's not going to behave like this all day."

Peter, however, had no intention of relenting. True, he followed them into the Kremlin and across the cobblestones towards Cathedral Square without straying more than a few

80

yards from their side. But he walked straight past the wonderful white Bell Tower of Ivan the Great, and showed no interest at all when Stephen pointed to the Tsar Kolokol, the world's biggest bell, despite its being over twenty feet high; nor did he laugh with Holly when Stephen explained that it had never worked, or feel compelled to touch the huge crack caused by a fire two years after its completion. He wasn't even interested in the Tsar Cannon with its huge cannon balls that no one had ever fired for fear that it would blow up. He just turned away from the awesome sights and plodded doggedly down the footpath leading to Cathedral Square.

While Holly exclaimed at the domes and cupolas of the buildings and listened, entranced, to Stephen's potted history, Peter stood alone in the centre of the square, scowling ferociously. Finally, Stephen and Holly ignored him, only checking that he was within view as they made a slow tour of the square, pausing occasionally to marvel at some particularly ornate piece of workmanship.

Holly looked back regretfully as Stephen finally led her away from the cathedral, past the Kremlin Palace to the Museum.

"We've already agreed on the Armoury for today—for Peter's benefit I seem to remember," he commented wryly.

Holly frowned as she waited for Peter to catch up. She was tempted to be very cross with him, but the memory of the previous day and his unexpected storm of tears still haunted her. She remembered, too, his earlier claim that he never cried, and decided he was angry that she had seen how unhappy he really was.

She smiled as he reached her side and asked warmly, "Ready for the Armoury?"

He nodded, his eyes slightly less hostile, but when Stephen spoke to him he turned away, hunching his shoulders and refusing to listen.

Holly frowned. So he was jealous of Stephen. Perhaps today hadn't been such a good idea after all.

"Stop dawdling or we'll be queuing all morning," Stephen called, his face red and shiny from the cold.

"Coming." Holly put her arm round Peter and walked briskly towards the queue waiting outside the Kremlin Museum. Although she felt him stiffen, she kept her arm determinedly round him, and by the time they reached the head of the queue he was more relaxed. Consequently, their trip round the Armoury was considerably more successful than their tour of Cathedral Square; the backless overshoes insisted upon and supplied by the museum management even drawing a slight smile from him as he thrust his sturdy boots into a small pair.

They left their coats in the cloakroom and padded across the slippery bees-waxed parquet floors to the first room, where an incredible array of pre-twentieth century battle gear was jammed into every available space. From there they passed through to the Trophy Room which displayed the fifteen thrones belonging to various Tsars. They all looked decidedly uncomfortable, despite their splendour, but even Peter was impressed by the diamond throne which was studded with two thousand diamonds and amethysts. He also liked the double throne used by the twin Tsars, Ivan and Peter, with its cut-out back section.

"It's said that their eldest sister used to hide behind the drapes in the cut-out space and whisper the right responses to her brothers when they held court," Stephen said with a laugh. "She was obviously a feminist in a city where royal women were rarely seen and even less heard."

Holly was delighted by his knowledge, her imagination already fired with colourful scenes at court. Each succeeding room added to her excitement—the Room of Crowns, the State Coach Room, the Silver Room, it went on and on. They saw some delightful oddities too, like Peter the Great's boots, which were almost as tall as little Peter—not so surprising in view of the Tsar's massive six feet eight inch frame.

Then they admired a horse robe made from the feathered skins of five hundred yellow parrots, and the Clock of Glory, made for Catherine the Great.

"*Once a mechanical eagle dropped pearls into the beak of its young every five seconds, music played and a waterfall sprang to life*," Holly read from her guidebook. "See the baby eagles, Peter. Aren't they marvellous?"

"I liked the ivory eagle best." He was referring to an ornately carved figure of a bird perched on a rock of ironwood that they had seen a little earlier.

"Yes, I liked that one too," she agreed, glad that he was at last responding.

"Aren't you hungry yet?" Stephen asked as he caught up with them. "I didn't realise you'd be this enthusiastic. We've been walking for hours so it's way past my lunchtime"

Holly gave him an apologetic smile. "I've been dreadfully selfish, I'm afraid. And there's still so much to see."

"Well, it will have to wait for another day. My stomach is becoming an embarrassment." Stephen shook his head in mock reproof. "I think it's time we made for the nearest restaurant, right, Peter?"

"Right." Surprisingly, Peter responded with a smile.

"Come on then." Stephen led the way back to the cloakroom, winking at Holly as he did so.

They left the Kremlin via Trinity Gate and headed towards the nearest luncheonette. Stephen's Russian was not as fluent as Dirk's, but the self-service cafeteria didn't call for much expertise and Holly piled hot pies and potatoes onto two plates for herself and Peter, while Stephen chose a *kotleta,* a sort of fried meat patty.

They found themselves a table and were soon eating. The worst of his hunger appeased, Stephen announced, "That's better. Now I can concentrate on plans for the rest of the day? How about the circus?"

"The circus!" Peter cried, through a mouthful of potato.

"I don't see why not," Stephen told him. "Especially as I just happen to have three complimentary tickets and the show starts in about an hour."

* * *

The circus was the turning point, with Peter reverting to the laughing child of the previous day, clapping wildly at the tame bears, and staring in wide-eyed disbelief at the antics of the Cossack riders.

"I don't know how to thank you," Holly told Stephen as she watched her charge laughed hysterically at a tumbling clown.

"You don't have to," he replied, covering her hand with his own. "After all, I wouldn't have had much fun alone. In fact, I can't think of anyone I'd rather share a day with."

"Does that include Peter?" she asked, trying unsuccessfully to withdraw her hand.

"Even Peter. And don't try to get away because you won't succeed. I'm not asking for a grand affair, Holly, just friendship and its simple pleasures. England is a long way away, you know."

"How long have you been in Moscow?" she asked, struck by his tone of voice.

"Six months," he admitted, "and sometimes it gets very lonely."

"But what about all the diplomatic functions you have to attend? The parties and receptions. I thought it was a glamorous job."

"So does everybody." He clapped enthusiastically as the clown finished his act. "But I'm too junior for a lot of the functions—and, besides, they become very repetitive, and they are not that much fun if you have to attend on your own."

"But surely there are girls at the Embassy?"

"None that I fancy. And that reminds me: will you be my guest at an Embassy dinner in two weeks' time? It's a fairly informal affair."

"I don't think I ought to," Holly began. "Mr. Van Allen might…"

"I'm sure he won't mind," Stephen interrupted her. "He's always telling me to find myself a partner."

Holly shelved the problem. "I'll come if you can clear it with him," she promised, sure that Dirk would refuse his request in view of his recent threat that she leave Stephen alone.

"Great." He seized her hand again and gave himself up to the delights of the circus, oblivious to Peter's fresh scowls.

* * *

It was late when they reached the apartment, and Peter was very tired. Holly had insisted on paying for a taxi and once inside it he had lolled against her shoulder like a rag doll.

Stephen left them at the entrance, and she supported a rather tottery Peter up the stairs. She was just pushing her key into the lock when the door opened sharply, pitching her straight into Dirk's arms.

"Where on earth have you been?" he asked furiously. "It's so late that I was just deciding which hospital to telephone first."

"We've been to the circus," Holly replied coolly. Then, staging an attack of her own, "Last night you made it very clear to me that Peter was entirely my responsibility, so when the opportunity to visit the circus arose, I didn't think I had to ask your permission."

"There is such a thing as common courtesy." Dirk gave her a look of cold disapproval. "But we can discuss that later. In the meantime I suggest that you hurry up and put Peter to bed? He's almost asleep standing up."

"I have every intention of doing so." Holly threw off her coat and then undid Peter's buttons. Although he stood motionless and sleepy-eyed, there was something close to satisfaction in his expression. She frowned slightly, wondering if he was glad they had made Dirk angry. Then, noting the circles round his eyes she dismissed the thought from her mind and led him through to his bedroom.

He was asleep almost as soon as his head touched the pillow, and she tucked him in with a sad smile. Dirk could be as angry and unreasonable as he liked about the lateness of the hour; the visit to the circus had been a Godsend. From the moment the clowns tumbled into the ring he had reacted like any normal five-year-old and for that she was grateful.

She closed the bedroom door quietly behind her, intending to make herself a hot drink and go straight to bed. Dirk, however, had other ideas. He called to her from the sitting-room. With Peter's dirty socks still in one hand, she paused in the doorway, expecting more unpleasantness.

"Holly, I'd like you to meet Melina, Comtesse de Carcassonne. As Melina often visits the apartment, it will be as well if you get to know one another." Dirk's voice was bland and entirely reasonable as he turned to his guest. "Melina, this is Holly Williams, Peter's new nanny."

The Comtesse narrowed her very beautiful green eyes and stared across at Holly. Despite her name, she was American and she spoke with a pronounced drawl.

"But we've met before, haven't we, honey?"

Holly could only nod dumbly, horrified at this sudden turn of events as her past came back to haunt her. Melina, a rich widow who lived a ridiculously flamboyant lifestyle, had only been invited onto Holly's television chat show at the last moment to replace a celebrated film producer suddenly struck down with flu. With little time to prepare, and nothing about the Comtesse de Carcassonne in her notes except that her dead husband had been thirty years her senior, the programme had been a disaster.

Not from the viewers' point of view, admittedly, as they had enjoyed the fracas—but for Melina, who had found herself attacked on every side by her fellow guests: two members of a third world action group, the director of a large charity, a missionary, and the parents of a handicapped child who were trying to raise money for a special wheelchair.

She had come out of the programme very badly, her huge wardrobe and much publicised extravagance an obscenity beside the material deprivation that formed the main theme of the show.

Holly's subsequent sincere apology had done little to appease Melina, who had left London threatening all kinds of retribution.

"Relax, Holly, she won't do a thing," the producer had soothed her. "I know she should never have been invited, and the researcher concerned has had her knuckles sharply rapped. Apparently she confused Melina with the previous Comtesse, a lady well-known for her philanthropy. Still, she's hardly going to draw further attention to herself after last night's fiasco, is she? So forget it. We'll never hear from her again."

Nor had they, although Holly had sometimes woken at night in a cold sweat thinking about the programme and wondering if she could have directed the conversation more tactfully. Then, with Martin's illness, the whole affair had been forgotten, her career abandoned. Now it all came back to her and, looking across at Melina, Holly realised that her past was about to catch up with her with a vengeance. The American was still as beautiful, still as perfectly groomed, and still as angry. It was abundantly clear from her scowl that she hadn't forgotten a single moment of the television programme, and she was going to make Holly pay with interest.

* * *

"You've already met?" Dirk said in surprise. "How extraordinary. I wouldn't have thought you moved in the same circles."

"We don't!" Melina snapped, and then, aware that her display of bad temper was unbecoming, she forced a smile. It didn't reach her eyes, however, and they glittered, cold and green as a winter sea as she turned back to Holly.

"You've obviously had your reasons for changing your career. I just hope, for Dirk's sake, that you're a better nanny than you were a television presenter. Or perhaps—" she paused, enjoying her revenge— "perhaps you didn't have a choice at all. Perhaps you messed up a programme once too often."

"I really don't see..." Holly began, dismayed by their confrontation, but the American interrupted her.

"Well, it's about time you did see. My appearance on your two-bit show cost me half a million dollars; the price I had to pay in charitable donations to repair the damage to my reputation."

"But that's so generous." Holly took a step forward, her face lighting up. It hadn't been such a disaster after all, not if it had persuaded Melina to use some of her vast wealth to help the poor and underprivileged.

"Maybe." Melina smiled for Dirk's benefit then her face darkened again. "But I disliked being made to look a fool."

"I already explained the mistake," Holly pleaded, "and so did my producer. And it was so long ago that I'm sure everybody else has forgotten about it. If the viewers remember anything at all it will be about your generosity."

Melina refused to be mollified. Instead, she turned to Dirk. "Just be careful she doesn't stab you in the back. She's capable of anything."

Dirk stared across at Holly, his face grim. "Am I to understand that you are a television presenter as well as a writer?"

"Was," Holly corrected him, her heart sinking when she saw the expression in his eyes. "I stopped hosting my television show a long time ago when…when I decided to become a writer," she finished lamely, unable to put the truth into words in the face of his hostility.

He continued to stare at her as he addressed the comtesse. "What show are you talking about, Melina?"

"My goodness, are you really telling me you didn't know, darling?" Melina raised her eyebrows triumphantly. "Has Miss Williams pulled a fast one again and forgotten to tell you about her past?"

"What show?" Dirk repeated.

"*'Goodnight London'* of course, although you've probably never watched it. It's hardly your sort of thing."

Dirk ignored Melina and advanced on Holly, his eyebrows a straight line of fury across eyes that glittered dangerously.

"So you're Harwyn Williams are you? I thought you looked familiar when we first met but dismissed it as mere imagining. I suppose Holly is just a convenient pseudonym to prevent suspicion. No wonder you know so much about me. You've probably watched every news clip I ever featured in, just to get your facts right."

"That's not true." Holly took a step backwards as she faced his ice-cold anger. "Harwyn Williams is both my real and my professional name, but I've always been called Holly by my family and friends. Besides I don't work in television anymore."

"No, because you've turned to prose instead." Dirk's eyes were full of contempt. "What was your brief? To dig up as much dirt as possible about me in particular, and the diplomatic corps in general? I know we're meant to be a dying breed in the light of today's satellite communications but we're still human, Miss Williams. And people don't like having their trust betrayed."

"I've already told you the truth." Holly was both upset and angry. "I'm doing research for a book, a historical novel set in Moscow. Nobody sent me here."

"And your journalistic instincts won't be tempted by the odd spicy anecdote, I suppose?" Dirk gave a bitter laugh. "Come off it Harwyn Williams. I seem to remember you winning several awards, and your occasional newspaper articles were a byword in clever sleuthing."

"Only someone with something to hide ever felt threatened by me," Holly said firmly. "My journalism was always honest."

"Not according to Melina."

"Did you watch the programme?" Holly glared back at him, her face pale but composed. She was quite certain that he intended to dismiss her and send her back to London and she had no intention of going without a fight.

"I didn't but surely Melina's word is enough." She saw the faint flicker of doubt in his hazel eyes.

"Hardly!" She took another step backwards and put her hand on the door. Then, holding herself steady, she addressed them both. "Because her public image suffered, the Comtesse de Carcassonne will always blame me, but I'm afraid it was largely her own fault. I became a television presenter on the strength of my journalism; I wasn't a personality, merely a sounding board for other people's ideas. Madame la Comtesse made a fool of herself when she appeared on my programme, and you're about to do the same by believing her." She gave Dirk a pleading look.

"How dare you!" Melina gave a gasp of fury. "You're nothing but a cheap scandalmonger; someone who dredges up whatever dirt they can in the name of entertainment."

"You're wrong." Holly shook her head, her fingers tightening on the door handle. "I have never been anything other than an interviewer, and if the questions I asked you forced you to part with half a million dollars to help people who have nothing, then it's something I'm proud of, not something I regret. Now, if you'll both excuse me, I'll say good night."

She turned away, expecting an angry retort from Dirk, but silence followed her exit from the room and she had made it to her bedroom before Melina's indignant high-pitched tones were overlaid by Dirk's deeper response.

She closed and locked the door behind her with trembling fingers. Then she sank on to the bed in despair, tears of reaction trickling down her cheeks. To meet Melina de Carcassonne, one of the few mistakes of her brief but highly successful television career, was almost more than she could bear, following so soon upon her arguments with Dirk and having to deal with Peter's difficult behaviour.

Chapter Six

Surprisingly, Dirk wasn't in when she woke the following morning, heavy-eyed and pale from an anxious night. Nor did he return at lunchtime. Peter was already in bed by the time she finally heard his key in the lock. She braced herself as he approached the sitting-room, and greeted him nervously.

"Hello. Peter is already in bed—he was tired after last night."

"Hardly surprising. He must have been exhausted. I imagine you've had a difficult day with him?"

"Not really." Holly crossed her fingers behind her back as she answered him, remembering Peter's moods and silences. Anyway, it wasn't exactly a lie: he hadn't been naughty, only distant and melancholy, not wanting her to read to him, not interested in his food. She had been glad when bedtime came, glad finally to be alone. She needed to think about Dirk's possible reaction to Melina's disclosure.

In retrospect, she could hardly blame him for his suspicions of her; after all he was followed from party to party by the gutter press so her own reporting past would immediately put him on the defensive. She took her courage in both hands.

"About last night," she began. "I'd like to try and explain things."

"Don't bother to compound your lies. I think the least said the better, don't you? After all, we're stuck with one another for the time being, and that's bad enough without continuing what can only be a pointless discussion."

Holly was speechless, her mouth half-open in unspoken protest as he continued, "But just let me make one thing clear—I don't like journalists. Too often they expose private wounds and destroy people's lives so if I ever find out that you've printed so much as a single word about me or Peter, I'll sue you for impersonation with intent to deceive, to say nothing of defamation of character and libel."

Holly found her voice and answered him angrily. "I have no intention of writing about you nor, whatever Melina has told you to the contrary, did I ever intend to. I'm here to act as Peter's nanny and do some research for my book, nothing else. However, in view of your attitude, I think it would be better if you would arrange for a replacement as soon as possible. In the meantime, I'll endeavour to look after Peter satisfactorily."

"Oh no you don't." Dirk slammed the glass of whiskey he had been holding down on the table. "I refuse to be put to the expense and inconvenience of finding yet another nanny so you can return to London. Your initial contract is for six months, so that's how long you will stay here."

Holly interrupted him scornfully. "If it's only the expense that's bothering you, I'll gladly pay my own air fare."

"You, or the newspaper that's employing you?" He gave a short laugh. "I admire you for keeping up the pretence, Holly, but don't bother. Your contract is for six months and, in view of the surprising fact that Peter likes you, I expect you to honour it in full."

"And if I refuse?" Holly's eyes glinted angrily.

"Then I'll sue you for breach of contract as well. And please don't try my patience any further because, thanks to you, I've already lost Mrs. Malpass and had to deal with a hysterical Comtesse de Carcassonne. Now, if you'll excuse me, I have to dress for dinner as I'm going out."

* * *

Her brief confrontation with Dirk set the pattern for the next few days. He was rarely in and when they did meet, his manner was icily polite, as if his earlier interest in her had never existed. Holly responded with a similar coolness and concentrated instead on Peter, taking him to the planetarium and the puppet museum, and deciding to postpone her research for a short while as she attempted to cement their friendship.

He responded with wide-eyed interest as they entered the round planetarium and found themselves in a darkened universe filled with stars and shooting comets. And the visit to the puppet museum, followed by the treat of a matinée performance, kept them both amused for days as they attempted to make their own theatre from several cardboard boxes and a generous amount of paint. A second trip to G.U.M. furnished them with off-cuts of material, cotton and glue, and they soon had several hand puppets with which to act out nursery rhymes and fairy stories.

The difference in Peter was startling; he stopped his unpredictable silences and began to laugh freely. Mealtimes found him hungry and prepared to help cook if it meant that Holly would be free to play with him that much sooner. He was even friendly towards Stephen on the odd occasion that he dropped in for a cup of coffee, and Holly welcomed the change in his behaviour.

Despite the difficulties in her relationship with Dirk, she found herself enjoying Peter's company. She was refreshed rather than tired by the total concentration demanded of her by their puppet project.

"You're actually enjoying all this, aren't you?" Stephen said as he admired their latest puppet. "The new Holly Williams, puppeteer and child exploiter. How many hours has Peter worked on this project of yours?"

Holly laughed and poured him a second cup of coffee. She enjoyed his visits and the easy relationship that had sprung up between them. Somehow Stephen's youth and the fact that tragedy had never touched him made him relaxing company. She found that she laughed a lot when she was with him, something she had once felt to be impossible ever again.

"By the way," he told her on one of his visits, "that dinner I invited you to. It's next Friday, eight o'clock, cocktail dress."

"You mean Mr. Van Allen doesn't mind?" Holly was surprised but pleased. "In that case, I'll look forward to it. Puppets do have their limitations when it comes to intelligent conversation you know."

They walked together to the door, Stephen shrugging himself into a heavy sheepskin coat. He buttoned it up as Holly opened the door, and then started searching through his pockets.

"I must have left my gloves in the office although I could have sworn they were in my coat. I always seem to be losing things these days; I lost about twenty roubles last week, and a small pocket camera when we went to the circus. My own fault for being careless, I suppose, but it's very annoying."

"Perhaps the gloves will stop the pattern." Holly was sympathetic. "After all, misfortune is supposed to go in threes, isn't it?"

"Always the optimist," Stephen ruffled her hair in an affectionate parting gesture. "Don't forget, eight o'clock Friday," he said as he turned away—and then his voice changed to more formal tones as Dirk and Melina mounted the stairs.

Dirk's greeting was brief and he gave Holly a curt nod as she held the door open; Melina, however, was much more communicative. She glanced at Holly's untidy hair with a meaningful smile.

"Hardly the thing, darling," she drawled. "I don't think your employer's doorstep is really the place for amorous farewells."

Holly spluttered in indignation but before she could answer Melina swept by, wafting an expensive perfume in her wake. Dirk helped her out of her coat, effectively

95

trapping Holly in the hallway. His face was full of polite interest as Melina chattered about the reception they had just attended, but he didn't offer any comment. Despite her own irritation with him, Holly found herself wondering just how interested he really was in Melina's bitchy remarks about the other guests.

She glanced up at him as Melina entered the sitting-room, leaving Dirk to hang up her fur coat. For a second, as their eyes met, she glimpsed his loneliness and boredom, then the moment passed and his eyes grew as hostile as they travelled the length of her body with slow deliberation, from her tousled hair and back again. Defensively, she raised her hand and attempted to smooth her lopsided topknot, cursing Stephen silently as she did so.

"Don't bother," he said with a mirthless smile. "It's beyond repair."

"It isn't what you think," Holly said, still smarting from Melina's insinuation. "We were just—"

"I don't need a blow by blow account of your activities, Holly." Suddenly he laughed, a harsh bitter sound. "Stephen's constant good humour these days makes your relationship painfully obvious. In fact, I've been meaning to thank you. I was mistaken when I tried to warn you off—he's gone from strength to strength since his involvement with you. You seem to have given him a new interest in his work and, after all, he has to start somewhere."

"How dare you!" Holly was white with anger. "How dare you try to spoil a perfectly innocent friendship? Surely even you are not so obtuse that you can't see that Melina is out to cause trouble? How can you possibly believe her stupid insinuations?"

"Shall we leave Melina out of this?" Dirk took a step towards her. "After all, I don't need anything other than my own eyes to tell me that Stephen has changed, and when you stand on the doorstep with your hair in a mess, it doesn't take long to draw the right conclusion."

96

"You're despicable." Holly flung the words at him, her face tight with anger. "You judge everyone by your own standards, don't you? Well let me tell you that not everybody is like you. A lot of people are actually prepared to be friends without any sexual involvement—and Stephen is one of them. Now, if you'll excuse me, I'm going to bed."

She pushed past him in the direction of her bedroom, angry tears sparkling on her cheeks.

"Holly?" She heard the query in his voice and then one arm was round her waist while his free hand tilted her chin upwards. "You're crying."

"What else do you expect?" she stormed, her fists pounding his chest. "Do you think that being an ex-journalist makes me so hard-boiled that I can take every insult on the chin? Well, it may interest you to know that I can't. I've had enough. First Mrs. Malpass jumped to too many conclusions, then Melina made her unfair accusations and you believed them, and now you are intent on smirching the only real friendship I've made in Moscow. Stephen is good and kind and..."

"Not the man for you." Suddenly Dirk's mouth was on hers, plundering her lips, draining her of strength so that she clutched weakly at his coat.

For a moment time stood still and his kiss was the only reality, warm and demanding, reminding her of needs she had long ignored. Melina's voice dragged them apart, her irritation carrying clearly from the sitting-room.

"What are you doing Dirk? I'm dying for a drink, sweetheart."

Aghast, Holly stared at him. How could he kiss her with his current girlfriend only a room away? And, even more horrifying, how could she respond when only a week earlier she had been convinced that Darren had killed all her desire for physical love forever? How could Dirk, whom she didn't even like, reduce her to trembling acquiescence with one unexpected kiss?

97

"I'm sorry. I shouldn't have done that." He stared down at her, his hands still firm on her waist.

"No, you shouldn't. Now let me go" Holly tried to pull herself from his arms. "Just leave me alone, and go to Melina. She's calling you again."

Melina was doing more than calling because, as Dirk reluctantly let Holly go, she appeared in the sitting-room doorway, a petulant frown on her face.

"Whatever are you doing?" she began, and then broke into an affected smile. "Hello, honey, you must be Peter. Come here and tell me all about yourself."

* * *

The next hour passed in a daze. Holly didn't know if Peter had seen her in Dirk's arms any more than she knew why she had kissed him, and she found it difficult to concentrate as she helped her charge set up the puppet theatre.

Surprisingly, Peter seemed to like Melina, and was eager that she should see his puppet theatre. A ten-minute display of puppetry was more than enough for Dirk, however, and he interrupted Melina's extravagant praise.

"Right, Peter, time for bed. You can show us your puppets again another day."

Peter put up a token protest but his eyelids were drooping and he allowed Holly to lead him back to his bedroom without a fuss. In two minutes he was asleep, his lashes a dark fringe against his cheeks. Sighing, Holly pushed herself up from the bed and returned to the sitting-room to tidy up the puppet theatre.

"Very ingenious of you." Melina's words of praise took her unawares. "It must be so difficult to amuse a poor motherless child. I expect he misses her dreadfully." Her eyes fixed on the portrait of Isabella above the fireplace. "He looks very like her, doesn't he? One would hardly believe him to be Dirk's son, he's so small and dark."

98

Holly nodded silently as she gathered up Peter's puppets and headed for the door.

"I expect you're tired," Melina continued solicitously. "Caring for small children is exhausting—but rewarding, of course, particularly with such an enchanting child."

Holly knew she was trying to gain Dirk's favour through his nonexistent paternal instincts, but she was too tired to smile. Instead, she turned away. Let Melina try to tame Peter and Dirk if that was what she wanted. She was obviously on the lookout for a new husband and Dirk probably suited her on all counts, being not only handsome and rich but many years younger than the elderly husband who had left her his fortune. As for Peter, he had been pushed from nanny to nanny for too long to have any serious objections to a new mother. Indeed, he appeared attracted by Melina, and had sat very close to her, too young to recognise that her interest would soon wane once it had served its purpose.

Dirk didn't smile either, he merely opened the door for Holly, his eyes shuttered and cold. It was clear that Melina's reference to Isabella, and her observations about Peter's resemblance to his dead mother had been enough to remind him of the past he was constantly trying to forget by kissing any female who was available whether they wanted him to or not.

* * *

Holly put on a clean nightdress and brushed her teeth, but when she climbed into bed she could no longer control her thoughts. She felt hot and feverish at the memory of Dirk's arms around her. She threw back the bed covers and crossed the room to open the tall double-glazed window a fraction, and let in a brief gust of fresh air.

The memory of Dirk's lips, soft and questioning, not taking but giving, followed her back to her cold bed. She pulled the covers round her shoulders and curled into a ball,

99

sure she was reading something into his actions that wasn't there?

She lay dry-eyed in the darkness, reliving her body's unexpected treachery. Why had she responded so readily? Was it just that Dirk was a very practised seducer, or was it something more? Panic-stricken, she closed her eyes tightly, willing herself to sleep.

* * *

She was brought out of a half sleep by a loud crash, followed by the tinkle of falling glass. The noise seemed to be in the room with her and she screamed, knocking over her bedside lamp in her fear of being trapped in the darkness with an unknown intruder.

She rolled away from the bed and groped her way towards the door, praying that she would reach it safely. The crack of light under it seemed impossibly distant as she banged her leg on a jutting cupboard and bit back a moan of pain.

Dirk's voice came as a relief for once. "Holly!" He tried to open the door, rattling the handle. "Holly, are you all right?"

She couldn't answer him, paralysed with the fear of what might be in the room with her.

"Holly. Can you unlock the door? Holly, answer me."

He didn't wait for her reply but threw himself against the panelling so hard that the door shuddered on its hinges.

The noise brought Holly to her senses. She covered the last few feet in a rush, and turned the key in the door. It burst open, flooding the room with light, and she almost fell into Dirk's arms. He held her close, giving her time to calm down, and after a moment she noticed that he had removed his tie and that his shirt was open at the front. She could also smell Cognac on his breath but it didn't matter. All she wanted was to be safe.

"What's the matter? Have you hurt yourself?" He tightened his arms around her, his voice full of concern.

"There…was a noise…in my room! I think someone is in there," she quavered.

Gently, he put her to one side and stepped through the doorway, switching on the light as he did so. He was back in a moment.

"It's all right. You left your bedroom window open and the outside window has smashed the inner one. It's one of the hazards of Russian winds and this style of double glazing, I'm afraid. I should have warned you only to use the tiny trap window at the top."

"Is that all?" She gave a sigh of relief and held on to the door frame, trying to control her trembling. "I thought someone had broken in."

"You've been reading too many crime novels." Dirk gave a slight smile which quickly changed to an expression of concern as her teeth began to chatter. Stepping back into the room, he pulled a blanket from the bed and wrapped it tightly around her. Then he led her to the sitting-room, his arm still on her shoulders.

He poured her a brandy, "Drink this while I do something about your window. If we leave it open to the air for very long, your bedroom will be like an ice box."

Holly took the drink with trembling fingers and sat close to the electric fire.

"Will you be all right on your own?" he asked.

She nodded, wishing he would put a jumper on, anything to hide the broad expanse of his chest. Her fright had faded, leaving her feeling slightly foolish, but she couldn't control the spasmodic shivering of her body and she knew it wasn't entirely due to shock.

* * *

When he returned, fifteen minutes later, he held out his hands to the fire. "Fortunately the outside window wasn't damaged so I've closed it. I've cleared up the glass from the inner pane and pulled a few dangerous splinters from the frame. Tomorrow I'll arrange for someone to come and mend it. In the meantime the curtains are heavy enough to keep out any draughts and I've given you an electric heater as well."

"Thank you." Holly was relieved to see that he had pulled on his Guernsey sweater. "I'm sorry I disturbed you."

"You didn't." He indicated her brandy glass with a wry smile. "I was just about to indulge in some serious drinking, so your interruption was a blessing in disguise."

He laughed at her embarrassment. "Have I offended you, Miss Williams? Would it be easier to pretend that I don't have any bad habits, like drinking in my bedroom or kissing unsuspecting nannies?"

"If you'll excuse me, I'd like to return to my room now." Holly pushed herself up from the chair.

"That's right. Retreat behind the safety of your locked door." Dirk rose, too, and took a step towards her.

In a sudden panic Holly turned away. As she did so she trod on the blanket, pulling it from her shoulders so that it fell in a bright yellow puddle at her feet. With a sharp intake of breath she bent to retrieve it, but Dirk was faster. He seized the blanket and lifted it back on to her shoulders, steadying it with his outstretched hands as he gazed down at her.

"Are you really that frightened of me, Holly? Do you honestly think I would take advantage of you if you didn't lock your bedroom door? Or perhaps you're locking something out? This, for example."

He lowered his head and claimed her mouth for the second time that evening but without moving his arms, so that she was trapped against him by the yellow blanket. His mouth was gentle as he moved his lips slowly across hers and then down the slender arch of her throat, however. Holly's legs felt like water as she swayed against him, unconsciously arching her neck and parting her lips, her eyes half-closed.

Instantly, he stopped and with one abrupt movement wrapped the blanket chastely about her. "Is that why you lock your bedroom door, Harwyn Williams? Are you really afraid of me—or am I just an excuse because you are actually afraid of yourself."

* * *

The next morning found Holly dreading a further confrontation with Dirk. His words the previous night had jolted her into an examination of her behaviour and although she had stormed from the sitting-room, she recognised the truth of his statement in the cold morning light.

All their arguments stemmed from a mutual attraction, a subconscious need. The fact that she despised Dirk's attitudes, and that he didn't trust her, made no difference. They wanted each other.

No, she wanted him, she corrected herself. Dirk wanted anything female and passably attractive, but she had rejected men since her disillusionment with Darren and had never seriously contemplated an involvement with anyone else. So why Dirk, and why now? She sighed as she dressed, wondering how she could extract herself from such an embarrassing situation. She couldn't leave Peter without a nanny, but on the other hand she had no intention of succumbing to her ridiculous emotions.

When she reached the kitchen, however, she found that fate had stepped in because there was a brief note from Dirk propped against the teapot. It stated that he had been called away on urgent business and wouldn't return until the weekend.

With a sigh of relief, she screwed it up and threw it into the trash. At least she had a few days' grace, and by the time the weekend arrived he would probably be concentrating on Melina again.

Stephen proved to be Holly's saviour while Dirk was away, dropping in every day with news and gossip, and frequently eating at the kitchen table with her and Peter so that she didn't have time to think about the future. His very normality helped her to push the memory of Dirk's kisses to the back of her mind, as did the trip he organised to Durov's Corner, Moscow's miniature zoo.

Holly was enchanted with the trained birds and animals. "I've never seen anything like it," she whispered between acts. "How do you think they train them?"

"The way you train Peter, with kindness and bribery," Stephen teased. "By the way, you haven't forgotten our dinner date on Friday, have you?"

* * *

Stephen arranged for a babysitter to arrive at a quarter to eight on Friday evening. She proved to be a stout motherly person who quickly dispelled Holly's doubts by offering to read Peter a bedtime story. Holly gave her a grateful smile and then hurried to answer the door for a second time as Stephen arrived.

"Wow!" His eyes widened at the sight of her. "I'll be the man everybody loves to hate."

"Don't be silly," Holly said, laughing. "On the other hand—" she fluttered her eyelashes in an exaggerated fashion— "perhaps you can be just a bit silly. It does wonders for my ego."

Stephen offered her his arm with a grin, and they strolled down the stairs and the few hundred yards to the Embassy, chatting amiably.

Most of the guests had already arrived, and Holly found herself running a gauntlet of stares. She took a deep breath and switched on the smile she had perfected for her television programme. Unfortunately, it didn't seem to have its usual effect—well, not entirely. Several men smiled back but most of the women looked away and started talking amongst themselves.

104

Her smile became fixed as Stephen led her across the room, and when he introduced her to several people beside the bar she told herself that she was imagining that their questions were more than mere idle curiosity. She tried to pull herself together, sure that she had merely forgotten what a large social gathering was like after several years of self-imposed isolation. Swallowing the rest of her drink, she accepted a second one as she tossed back her hair in defiance at the furtive glances around her. Maybe it was because she was a newcomer, someone not yet accepted into their inner circle. Looking around while Stephen chatted to someone about a work problem, she found herself staring directly into a pair of cold hazel eyes that left her in no doubt at all that their hostility was genuine.

Chapter Seven

"What the hell are you doing here?" Dirk asked furiously.

"Stephen invited me," Holly replied.

"Well, he should have had more sense." Dirk blocked her view of the room so that they were isolated into a corner. "I told him to keep an eye on you, not parade you through the Embassy."

Holly, startled by the vehemence in his voice, sprang to Stephen's defence.

"He said he'd cleared this evening with you. I asked him to because I was worried you might think it an unsuitable invitation for Peter's nanny."

"Damn!" He gave a low groan. "He did mention something last week but I forgot all about it. If I'd remembered, I'd have certainly changed my mind in view of the present circumstances."

"What circumstances?" Something in his tone told Holly that he was not referring to their own bitter truce but to something more serious. Before he could answer, however, Stephen returned, accompanied by two young men and a very pretty girl.

"Ah, Stephen." Dirk surprised Holly by producing an unexpected smile. "Thank you for looking after Holly for me. Fortunately I managed to leave Leningrad early after all, so I can relieve you of what I am sure was a very pleasant responsibility."

Stephen looked utterly bewildered but Dirk stepped smoothly into the ensuing silence.

"Holly, this is John Marshall, Simon Delaney and Sally Bingham. They all work in my department." He turned to Stephen's three companions. "I'd like you all to meet a very good friend of mine, Harwyn Williams, the well-known television presenter. She's in Moscow doing some research, and when she heard that I between nannies for Peter and that Mrs. Malpass was ill as well, she very kindly stepped into the breach."

"That was brave of you." Sally Bingham was a young graduate, new to the diplomatic service, and an ardent feminist who had no intention of ever joining the ranks of childminders.

"Not really." Holly tried to gather her thoughts. "Research is not like writing. In fact, I've quite enjoyed sharing Moscow with Peter. He's given me a fresh insight into modern Russia."

"What sort of book are you intending to write, Miss Williams?" One of the young men was looking at her with open admiration.

"A historical novel." Holly tried to sound enthusiastic and play the part that Dirk had cast for her. After all, she could hardly deny that she was Harwyn Williams. But she was at a loss to understand his sudden claim to friendship. As she continued to answer questions and ask some of her own, she saw Dirk lead Stephen to one side. They had a brief conversation and then Stephen, with a worried glance in Holly's direction, hurried away.

* * *

With an expansive smile, Dirk rejoined the group clustered around Holly. "I'm sorry to break this up but I promised to introduce Harwyn to several people who can help with her research."

"Perhaps we will have the pleasure of your company again later?" John Marshall's eyes were bright with curiosity.

"Not if I see you first," Dirk muttered under his breath as they turned away; then, aware of Holly's raised eyebrows, he gave a rueful grin. "Not one of my favourite people. He's a gossip, and a troublemaker, and someone you should avoid."

"For goodness' sake will you please tell me what this charade is all about?" Holly's patience was at an end. "I'm not your good friend, and neither do you intend to introduce me to people who can help with my research. That was just a ruse to remove me from John Marshall's sphere. Exactly what are you up to?"

"Saving your reputation." Dirk took her arm and directed her towards a large group of people. "Just play along with me," he whispered, tightening his grip. "It's for your own good."

Then, without giving her time to reply, he thrust her into the centre of the group and made the necessary introductions. Most of the older guests had watched *'Goodnight London'* several years earlier, and they greeted her with surprised pleasure.

"Of course, you were the interviewer who made Melina de Carcassonne look such a fool," one of the men in the group declared. "I was in Paris at the time, and her fury reverberated all the way across the channel."

"I'm afraid that was the result of a very unfortunate mistake on the part of the researchers," Holly replied diplomatically. "With different fellow guests, the Comtesse would have featured well; she is a very beautiful woman."

"But still a fool," the man who had spoken grinned disarmingly. "She led Jean-Pierre a terrible dance when she married him. I suspect he'd have lasted another ten years without her."

"Oh, come on, Jack, that's a bit cruel," Dirk cut in. "You know he was absolutely besotted with her—and she made his last years very happy by all accounts."

"And spent a great deal of his fortune into the bargain," Jack refused to be sidetracked. "Still, you can afford to be magnanimous, can't you?" He turned to the rest of the group for support and they joined in with his laughter. "At one time we thought the Comtesse had you earmarked as her next victim, but Miss William's timely appearance will probably get you off the hook. After all, you will hardly be her favourite man once she knows that you are friends with her public prosecutor."

"I don't think it was quite that bad," Dirk said urbanely. "And we really shouldn't discuss Melina behind her back; it's very uncharitable. Let's change the subject."

He began talking about his recent trip in general terms, and soon the other guests in the group were all proffering personal views on the difference between Leningrad and Moscow, and Melina was forgotten; but Holly gave Dirk several puzzled glances, curious as to the cause of his smug expression.

* * *

When dinner was finally called, Holly found herself sitting between Dirk and Stephen, and opposite a non-English speaking Russian.

"You arranged this, didn't you?" she hissed furiously at Dirk. "You sent Stephen to change the seating when we first arrived, so perhaps now you'll be kind enough to tell me what's going on. Why am I being introduced to everyone one minute, under heavy escort, of course, and then kept in isolation the next?"

"I already told you, it's for your own good." Dirk reached for a bread stick and broke it in half. "Melina has been spreading all sorts of scandal about you and, in view of Stephen's gaffe in bringing you here tonight, it was all I could think of on the spur of the moment. Once everyone realises who you really are, they will put her bitchiness down to sour grapes, revenge for that television programme."

Holly shook her head distractedly. "What could she possibly say about me that would interest anyone here?"

"She didn't need to say much." Dirk stopped smiling. "In an enclosed community like an Embassy, reputations are ruined very easily, and until this evening yours was almost beyond repair. How Stephen didn't pick it up, I can't imagine."

"He was probably too busy visiting me. What exactly has Melina been saying?"

Dirk leaned back as a waitress began to dish out the main course. "That you are considerably more than Peter's nanny—and I'm afraid that because of Mrs. Malpass' sudden departure, and my reputation, she didn't need to say much more."

Holly stiffened. What a fool she had been to think that he was only intent on saving her reputation when he was obviously just as concerned about his own. Her voice was sharp as she replied, "Now I understand. You mean that Melina has been implying that I am your mistress and, as it's rather infra dig to import such a luxury into an Embassy apartment, particularly one that belongs to your father-in-law, your next promotion is at stake—to say nothing of your social standing in the right circles—if you don't quash the rumours?"

"Is that what you think of me?" His brows drew together in a frown.

"What other conclusion should I draw?" Holly's voice rose slightly as she became more indignant. "After your recent accusation that I wangled the job as Peter's nanny to report on your every move, you're hardly likely to be concerned about me. Tell me one thing, though. Why has Melina suddenly decided to vent her spite on you?"

"I checked your story if you must know," Dirk told her. "I contacted the Foreign Office because I wasn't happy about your apparent deception, and their investigations confirmed that you haven't worked as a journalist for almost four years. They also sent me a telexed copy of a newspaper report printed the day after Melina appeared on your television programme. It didn't exactly endear me to Melina of course, especially when I suggested she owed you an apology, so now she's got it in for both of us, which is why you must go along with this charade."

110

Holly was speechless, not sure whether to be indignant or relieved by his admission. Before she could gather her thoughts, however, Dirk was claimed by his neighbour, a grey-haired woman in a vivid green dress.

She turned instead to Stephen, sitting moodily on her left side. He didn't smile when she spoke to him but just pushed the food round his plate, his face sullen and miserable.

"Why didn't you tell me, Holly?" he asked at last. "I feel such a fool."

She touched his sleeve. "I only know that Dirk has some notion that my—our—reputation is at stake. Apparently Melina…"

"I'm not talking about this evening," Stephen interrupted her impatiently. "I'm talking about your deception. Why didn't you tell me who you really are, and that you are a close friend of Mr. Van Allen's?"

"Because I'm not. I never met him until I arrived in Moscow—that's all part of this evening's deception. And I'm not Harwyn Williams any longer, either. I gave up my television career several years ago."

"Truly?" He looked slightly happier.

"Truly," Holly reassured him. "I've never lied to you Stephen, so can we please still be friends?"

"I've never stopped," he returned. "And as a punishment you can tell me about your television career and the celebrities you've interviewed."

"You mean you never watched my show," she teased him, glad to see his smile. "I suppose you were too busy doing your homework when I was broadcasting"

Stephen laughed aloud. "I like you, Harwyn Williams, but in view of my boss' prior claim, I think I'd better back off slightly."

"You're almost as bad as Melina," Holly said, pulling a face. "Haven't I just told you that he has no prior claim— or any claim at all for that matter."

111

"If you want to carry on believing that, then I suggest that you don't turn around right now and look at him." Stephen gave her a sardonic smile that made him look older than his years, and then began to talk to Sally Bingham on his left.

Intrigued by his remark despite herself, Holly turned back to Dirk. He was eating silently, making no attempt to engage anyone in conversation, apparently lost in his own thoughts. As she looked at him, however, he raised his eyes.

"Hello." His half smile was tinged with sadness. "Have you made your peace with Stephen?"

"Yes."

Dirk continued to stare at her. "So how do you feel now?"

"A fake, I guess. I haven't been Harwyn Williams for such a long time, and I haven't written anything worth printing for even longer. I'm being fêted for something so transient that I had almost forgotten it ever happened."

"Why did you stop? My report didn't say why you left your career at its very peak."

"I had personal problems." Holly was still unable to put into words the events of those terrible days when she first learned of Martin's leukemia.

Her mind went back to the months by his bedside, the unending games and stories, the tubes and needles. Her career hadn't mattered, had been nothing compared to Martin's life. Then, the gradual trickling away of hope. The final weeks when he had to stay in hospital; forcing a smile every day as she entered the ward, staying beside him on the worst nights until that last dreadful day.

She had only left him for a few hours, the nurses insisting that she get some sleep, and she had promised Martin that she would be back by two. The one o'clock news had alerted her, a newsflash detailing a hospital fire. Somehow she had known even then. Flinging on her coat in a panic, she had left her purse behind, and the taxi driver had argued with her about her fare until he'd seen her face.

By then the flames were visible, streaks of orange through the dense grey smoke.

It was too late, of course. The hospital staff had evacuated all the wards and the firemen had done a sterling job controlling the blaze, but two people had died: an old woman from shock, and Martin from smoke fumes too strong for his collapsing lungs.

Even when she had seen his body, small and pale and infinitely peaceful, she hadn't been able to rid herself of the memory of the fire, and the nightmares that followed all featured Martin screaming for her through the flames. The doctors assured her that he'd known nothing, had already lapsed into unconsciousness before the fire started, but she hadn't been able to rid herself of guilt. For weeks she had blamed herself for everything—for the leukemia, for his death—and even now she felt that she should have been with him. The doctor's assurance that even without the fire, he wouldn't have lasted through the night, was little comfort. He was her child and she had failed him.

* * *

Everything came back to her on a rising tide of memory as Dirk questioned her, and she felt the dizziness she hadn't experienced for so long begin to threaten.

His eyes were anxious. "Are you feeling OK?"

"I'm fine." She forced herself to smile. "It's just that this evening has been rather a shock. I thought I'd left Harwyn Williams far behind me."

"So Harwyn really is your name?"

"Yes, it's part of my Welsh ancestry." Holly drew a deep steadying breath and dragged herself away from her memories.

"And very suitable too for a television presenter. It's formality makes you sound unapproachable. I like Holly better."

"So did my brothers." Holly suddenly laughed as she remembered her childhood nicknames, the various shortenings of Harwyn before her family had settled for Holly.

"That's better." Dirk pushed his spoon into his meringue. "You have a lovely smile, you know, and yet you often look sad."

She didn't know how to answer him, so concentrated instead on her dessert, spooning up the meringue and strawberries in silence.

"You also look very beautiful tonight," Dirk said conversationally, his voice so matter-of-fact that she was surprised into looking at him.

To her chagrin, he was laughing at her. "Is a compliment so terrible, Holly Williams? I tell you that you have a lovely smile and you lapse into silence, and the word beautiful has you jumping like a startled fawn—to which, I might add, you bear more than a passing resemblance. Did you choose that coffee-cream dress with that particular motive in mind, or is it just a fortunate accident?"

Holly found herself mesmerised by his words. His gaze brought a flush to her cheeks as she recognised his deliberate seduction of her. Suddenly her silk dress seemed too flimsy, the neck too low. Dirk was mentally undressing her in a room full of strangers and with an inward shudder of something akin to anticipation, she remembered his kisses. Whatever was happening to her? Already he and Peter had turned her safe, uneventful life topsy-turvy, forcing her back into a world full of problems and heartache; and now Dirk appeared to be breaking through all her carefully guarded barriers, reminding her that she was still young and desirable.

"Please don't." She looked down at her dessert, no longer hungry. "Not here, Dirk."

"Well, that's an improvement on not anywhere. Can I take it that this is an invitation to a later meeting?"

114

"No, you can't." Holly's reply was vehement, her eyes sparkling with a rekindled fury. "You know very well that I didn't mean any such thing. And anyway—" she gave a tight smile— "I thought that you were intent on saving my reputation, not ruining it."

"Your public reputation," Dirk corrected, pushing a bowl of sugar towards her as the waitress poured coffee. "My personal inclination, and your private reputation, are just between us."

"You're impossible!" She exploded.

"Totally amoral," he agreed with a grin. "It makes me much more interesting."

Fortunately she was saved from having to reply by a commotion at the top table as the Ambassador rose to speak, and for some considerable time everybody concentrated on his speech, regardless of their native language. Holly listened politely but without much concentration, her eyes on Dirk as she turned towards the top table. Despite her fury at his teasing arrogance, she had to admit the attraction he held for her.

If only he wasn't so unpredictable; angry with her one minute, complimenting her the next. She suddenly wished she had left Moscow at the very beginning with her first doubts and returned to the dull safety of her home in London before Dirk became more than she could cope with.

As if he sensed her thoughts, he turned his head and their eyes met. Immediately the Ambassador's voice became no louder than a whisper against the thudding of her heart. Her mouth was dry and she licked her lips, her hand going unconsciously to her throat.

Dirk's eyes didn't leave her face. They travelled slowly down to her mouth and then back to her eyes. The movement was like a caress, the promise of a kiss.

They continued to gaze at one another, joining in automatically with the applause that ended the Ambassador's speech. Holly suddenly experienced a dizzying sensation of need. With only the movement of his eyes, Dirk had aroused emotions that she had denied for so long. Despite herself, she was responding to his blatant sensuality even while she recognised that he could no more help flirting than Peter could help his tantrums. It was a behaviour pattern that he used as a protection against his real feelings. To him she was just another pretty face.

Rationalising didn't help her, however, because somewhere between one breath and the next, he had become important to her; had filled the empty space in her heart. She stared at him in horror. Had she fallen in love with someone who was everything she despised: a bad father, a rake, unpredictable and autocratic? And on top of that, was he just playing with her as he sought oblivion from his unhappy memories?

She stared down at the table. What a fool she was. She was behaving like a silly schoolgirl instead of a woman who had already experienced more than her fair share of unhappiness.

* * *

"Take Holly on to the dance floor, Stephen, and keep an eye on her while I do my social bit." Dirk's voice interrupted her thoughts as he pushed back his chair.

Holly flashed him a look of indignation but it was lost on him as he turned away, leaving Stephen to escort her from the banqueting hall.

"Not exactly what I had planned for this evening," Stephen gave her a wry smile as he swept her on to the dance floor. "But cheer up, Holly. It could be worse."

"I just object to the armed guard."

"Nothing worse than a tooth pick, I promise. I think Mr. Van Allen is just anxious that you don't get trapped into saying the wrong things. He's working very hard to extricate you from Melina's claws."

116

"So I noticed." Holly stared over his shoulder to where Dirk was conversing with several middle-aged men. "I imagine he has to protect his household for his own good."

Stephen gave her a sharp glance. "I think you've got him wrong," he said gently. "He never cares a fig what other people think of him."

"Not even in diplomatic circles?" Holly shook her head in disbelief. "Come on, Stephen. I admire your loyalty but Dirk is just too obvious. I'm an embarrassment to him and he's covering up the best way he can."

Stephen's answer was interrupted by Simon Delaney, one of the young men she'd been introduced to earlier. He smiled engagingly as he asked to dance with her. "After all, Stephen sat next to you for the entire dinner so it's about time he showed a little generosity."

"I'd love to dance with you." Holly disengaged herself from Stephen's arms and then pulled a face as he gave a slight frown.

"Don't worry," she whispered, "I'll behave beautifully. You can tell Dirk that he hasn't a thing to worry about."

* * *

Released from Stephen's protective custody, Holly did in fact begin to enjoy herself. She found that she was in great demand as a dance partner, and managed one or two conversations in sign language with foreign dignitaries as well as skillfully fending off the inquisitive questions directed at her by several of the older women.

Stephen frequently returned to her side and managed several more dances, but he left her free to circulate and when they danced they didn't refer to Dirk again. Instead, they kept their conversation on the light, impersonal level that was the basis of their friendship.

As far as Dirk's behaviour was concerned, Holly might not have existed. He neither spoke to her nor looked at her, although she was frequently close to him, and while part of

117

her was amused by his deliberate disassociation as he worked hard at showing everyone present that their supposed friendship was purely platonic, she was also aware of a curious desolation. She tried to forget him but, as the evening progressed, her smiles became more brilliant, her conversation more animated, in a subconscious attempt to attract his attention. How could he flirt with her so blatantly at the dinner table, and then ignore her so completely?

She was trying to concentrate on an ageing American businessman who was intent on telling her his life story when, out of the corner of her eye, she saw John Marshall approaching. She stiffened, remembering Dirk's warning. He was one of the Embassy troublemakers, a young man likely to sniff out the truth behind her visit to Moscow. She gave him a cool smile, wondering if she could refuse to dance with him, but before he reached her she found herself in Dirk's arms as he swept her away from her American companion with an apologetic smile.

"I'm afraid that I've neglected my guest," he apologised. "You must let me claim her for the last two dances."

"Go right ahead, my boy," the elderly American replied, and turned to a group discussing a recent performance of *Prince Igor*.

* * *

"I suppose you expect me to thank you for beating the Embassy gossip to the starting post." Holly held herself rigid, trying to ignore her suddenly racing pulse. Dirk's arms around her had sensitised her body so that every nerve seemed to shriek with need.

"Don't talk." He ignored her remark, merely pulling her closer so that their bodies merged, each step an act of unison that made Holly flush with embarrassment. Surely everyone in the room could see the tension between them?

118

She tried to pull herself away. Dirk gave a sharp intake of breath as her body arched away from his embrace.

He looked down at her, his eyes suddenly dark. "Relax, Holly. Everybody is too busy having a good time to notice us now. The Cognac has blurred their perceptions."

"No." Her answer was a low moan of denial.

"Yes." His voice was a mere whisper of sound against the dance music. "We've been playing games for too long. Your need shows every time you refuse to look at me, every time you produce a smile brilliant enough to seduce the whole room. And I want you too, have wanted you since you first flirted with me."

He pulled her back into the circle of his arms as the music slowed for the last dance, his lips brushing her hair as he moved against her, and in that moment Holly was lost. Her long denied senses exploded into excitement as she forgot his reputation and his moodiness. She felt as disorientated as if she had stepped into an unknown world, and her lips trembled as she tried to smile.

"Enjoy the dance," he murmured, his voice like a caress. "It's only the beginning."

* * *

But it wasn't, because when they mounted the stairs to the apartment, their deliberate separateness more potent in its promise than Holly would have believed possible, the babysitter was waiting for them.

"I'm afraid that I haven't had a very good evening," she explained. "Peter seems very poorly. He's running a high temperature."

Holly was in the bedroom before the babysitter had finished speaking, leaving Dirk to thank her and order a car to take her home. All thoughts of the evening, of her feelings for Dirk, were forgotten as she felt Peter's forehead.

119

It was very hot and his eyes were bright as he stared up at her.

"I don't feel very well," he whispered.

"Never mind, darling. I'll give you a drink of lemon and sponge you down," Holly reassured him. "You'll feel much better in the morning."

He didn't, though. His temperature was worse, and he kept being sick as Holly sat with him. After a particularly bad bout she was searching through his clothes for another pair of pyjamas when Dirk came into the room, a frown of irritation on his face.

"That was Melina's secretary on the telephone," he said. "Something about a missing bracelet. She thinks she might have dropped it when she last visited the apartment."

"Continuing her smear campaign perhaps." Holly's voice was muffled as she rifled through Peter's clothes. "I expect…" Her voice stopped abruptly.

"What's the matter?" Dirk came closer, his annoyance still apparent. They hadn't spoken since the previous evening, and she was well aware that he thought she was using Peter's illness as an excuse to avoid him.

"Nothing." She unfolded a pair of clean pyjamas as she turned away from the cupboard. "I'm just very tired. I didn't manage to sleep at all last night because Peter was so restless."

"Well, grab some sleep now," Dirk commanded. "I shall be in my study for most of the day, catching up on paperwork. I can easily wake you if he calls."

"Perhaps I will." Holly admitted her weariness. "I'll just wash his pyjamas and settle him down." She unwrapped the blanket that was covering Peter and slipped his arms into a clean pyjama jacket, noting with growing alarm the heat from his skin.

"I think we ought to call a doctor," she said, turning back to Dirk. "He's still running a very high temperature."

He gave a disinterested shrug. "I'll telephone him, if you insist, but I think you're making a fuss about nothing. He's just suffering from a twenty-four-hour tummy bug."

Holly didn't answer him as she concentrated on tucking Peter into bed and, with an audible sigh of irritation, he left the room.

As soon as he'd gone she turned back to the cupboard and seized the items she'd found hidden beneath Peter's clothes. She wasn't sure what to do about them, but she knew that Peter was too ill to be questioned.

Chapter Eight

The doctor, when he arrived, was inclined to agree with Holly. "He's suffering from some form of gastroenteritis," he admitted. "And there's a danger of dehydration unless he keeps some fluid down. Try sips of water on a teaspoon every half-an-hour, that might do the trick. Otherwise I'll have to take him into hospital."

Holly was horror-stricken. "Just for a tummy bug?"

"It's his size as much as anything. He's very small and thin; no reserves to fall back on. I'd rather have him in hospital if he doesn't improve within the next twelve hours."

Dirk had been listening silently but now he interrupted. "You had better try and get a few hours' sleep in that case, Holly. I'll sit with him for a while. I'm quite capable of feeding him spoonsful of water."

"I must agree with Mr. Van Allen," the Embassy doctor said. "Two patients are twice as much trouble as one, and you do look very tired. May I suggest that you try and sleep until lunchtime?"

By then there was no improvement in Peter's condition, however, and Dirk reported that he had brought up every drop of water.

"He's being very brave," he told her in a grudging voice. "I didn't realise that he had so much grit."

"There are a lot of things you don't know about him," she retorted bitterly, worry making her angry. Then, not waiting for his reply, she hurried through to Peter's bedroom.

He was pale now, and clammy, with black circles around his eyes.

"Try a tiny sip of water," she coaxed. "Just a drop, Peter."

He shook his head, eyes dull and disinterested.

"Surely there's something we can do?" Dirk had followed her into the bedroom and she detected the note of concern in his voice.

"Perhaps if I moisten a cloth with water and bathe his lips? I'll fetch a clean handkerchief."

"I'll go." Dirk was already at the door. "Where shall I find one?"

"In my top drawer." Too late, Holly remembered what else was in the drawer. She was waiting pale-faced for Dirk when he returned, Melina's diamond bracelet dangling from his fingers.

"I imagine you have an explanation?" His voice was full of disbelief.

"Yes, of course," Holly answered, her throat suddenly dry as she registered the note of accusation in his voice.

"And for these too?" He produced Stephen's gloves and camera. "It seems that despite my Foreign Office report, Melina was right after all, and you did lose your job because of some disgrace, possibly petty pilfering. When she told me that you had left your television programme halfway through a series, I told her there had to be a perfectly good explanation. I didn't think for a moment that you'd lost your journalistic credibility. Now I realise that my trust was ill-placed. I actually called Melina a bitch at one point, but at least she was an honest bitch."

"You can't believe that I stole them," Holly's eyes were bright with anger.

"What other explanation is there?" Dirk threw the articles on to the bed. "I found them in your drawer, and nobody else has been in the apartment. Do you take me for an utter fool, Holly? Because I wanted to make love to you, I kept making allowances, ignoring Melina's warnings, believing that eventually I'd find the real person hidden beneath so many layers of inhibitions. That's why I was angry when I heard the rumours circulating about you, and was determined to suppress them. But I can't make any more allowances. You've completely betrayed my trust, and let down your agency as well."

Holly closed her eyes against his onslaught, fists tightly clenched in her lap. She didn't know whether to laugh or cry, didn't know how to cope with his bitter accusations. Some deep part of her, the intuition that had made her such a good television presenter, recognised his unhappiness, realised that he felt betrayed by her apparent dishonesty—but it was quickly submerged by her own pain. Dirk's lack of trust, his belief only in what his eyes told him, was like a slap in the face. Surely he had more perception than that?

She opened her eyes, the explanation half-forming on her lips, but one look at his face told her that it would be a waste of breath. In his eyes she was damned, and any attempt to transfer her guilt to a defenseless child would be treated with contempt.

"What are you going to do?" Her voice was expressionless.

"I'm going to buy you a ticket for the first available plane back to London." His eyes were cold, unforgiving. "And consider yourself lucky that I'm leaving it at that. As far as Melina is concerned her bracelet was found under a cushion, but Stephen will get a full explanation and a lecture on getting too involved with sophisticated older women."

"And nothing I can say will change your mind?" Holly's voice was equally cold, her anger rising at his injustice.

"Nothing." His expression was grim. "With luck I can book you onto this evening's flight."

"No!" Peter's voice was weak, a mere whimper of sound, but it cut through their argument like a knife.

With an exclamation of horror, Holly turned to him. How could she have forgotten that he was so ill? She took his hands, noticing with a lurch of her heart that they were like tiny white claws, the skin almost transparent.

"You mustn't go." Tears rolled down his cheeks. "If you go I'll die," he whispered.

"Hush, darling." She put a hand on his forehead, noting its cold clamminess and the sharp drop in his temperature with alarm. "Of course you won't die. Daddy will be here to look after you." She tried to make her voice convincing. "He can manage perfectly well without me. Why, I expect Mrs. Malpass will be back shortly too."

"That's right." Dirk moved closer to the bed and put out a tentative hand. "We'll soon have you right again, Peter."

The child shrank away from him, his face white and set.

"Go away!" They could both hear the hysteria in his voice. "You want me to die because I killed my mummy. I only want Holly. She won't let me die." He subsided into sobs, his face buried in the pillows. Holly lifted him in her arms.

"Of course Daddy won't let you die, he loves you very much. After all, if you died he wouldn't have anyone left, would he?"

"He would, he'd have Melina. That's why I took her bracelet. I wanted you to have pretty things like her, so he would like you best."

"And Stephen's camera and gloves?" Holly raised her eyes and met Dirk's horrified gaze with a sad smile.

"I took them for Daddy," Peter sobbed.

"Why?" Holly persisted, aware of the growing self-disgust on Dirk's face.

"Because I didn't like Stephen holding your hand. I wanted Daddy to hold it, like when we went skating."

"So did I." Suddenly Dirk was an explosion of movement as he sat on the bed and gathered Peter and Holly into his arms. "I hated him holding Holly's hand, too."

"You did?" Peter's voice was muffled as Dirk held him close.

"Yes. I was jealous, too, Peter, and jealousy isn't a very nice feeling. It makes us say and do all sorts of horrid things."

"Why?" Peter squirmed round so that he was leaning against Holly's shoulder. He stared up at his father, his eyes wide with sudden hope.

"Because I think it makes us temporarily insane." Dirk directed his gaze downwards and managed a smile. "You were jealous when you took Melina's bracelet; I was jealous when I was unkind to Holly."

"Is that why you're crying?" Some of the colour had come back into Peter's cheeks and he looked at Dirk with interest.

"No, I'm crying because I'm happy." Dirk didn't try to hide the tears that misted his eyes; instead he looked at Holly.

"Will you stay with Peter and me, even though we're both insanely jealous?"

Holly blinked back her own tears and nodded, her emotions in too much of a turmoil to speak. In the space of half a minute her world had changed from total collapse to the beginning of something she hardly dared face. Love and hope and a new future were all beckoning to her, together with all the fears and problems she had vowed never to face again.

"Kiss each other," Peter demanded, his strength returning minute by minute. "Kiss each other because then Holly will be my new mummy."

"How do you work that out?" The laughter returned to Dirk's face as he settled his arms more closely about them.

"Because daddies always kiss mummies," Peter replied with five-year-old logic. "And you must sleep in the same bed," he added, "because Holly has bad dreams."

"You've lost me now," Dirk told his son, "but don't worry—I'll gladly comply." He grinned as he noticed the pink flush colouring Holly's cheeks. "How many kisses does it take?"

"A million trillion." Peter's answer was so prompt that Dirk collapsed with laughter.

"Will one do for now?" he offered once he could keep a straight face. "I'll try to get around to the others later."

"OK." Peter nodded, his eyes wide with anticipation.

The laughter faded from Dirk's face as he turned to Holly and suddenly they both forgot the small figure sitting between them.

"I'm sorry." He pulled her gently towards him and with one thumb traced the outline of her lips. "Will you forgive me?"

Holly nodded, as breathless as if she'd been running in a race.

Dirk's lips brushed hers, softly at first and then harder and more demanding as his pent-up feelings overflowed. For a moment she was motionless as all the bitterness and unhappiness of her life flashed before her mind's eye. And then she was free to respond with an equal hunger, all her needs and her hopes for the future communicated with her lips and the restless movement of her hands as she pulled him closer.

"Me too," Peter interrupted them. "I want a kiss too."

Dirk and Holly broke apart and both kissed him simultaneously, their hands entwined and laughter in their eyes.

* * *

Much later, when Peter was almost asleep, worn out by the excitement but well on the road to recovery, Dirk slipped an arm round Holly's shoulders.

"It's time we had something to eat, young man," he told Peter. "We'll come back later, OK."

"Mmm." Peter's voice slurred with weariness as he turned over. "G'night."

"Good night, son." Suddenly Dirk bent and kissed him, his hand lingering for a moment on the dark head. Then he straightened up and smiled at Holly. "I've never called him that before."

"I had noticed."

She led the way from the bedroom and he closed the door quietly behind them. "It must have been difficult though, being left with a tiny baby whose birth killed your wife. I can understand your struggle to love him even though he loves you more than life itself. You know that, don't you? He might like me more than his other nannies, but it's you he wants."

"I know." In one swift movement Dirk stopped her, his arms so tight that he almost crushed her. Looking up at him Holly saw the anguish in his eyes and sighed. Would it always be like this? Would Isabella always intrude between them? Her sigh was a tiny whisper of sound, no more than a breath, but it Dirk heard it.

"You've got me as wrong as I got you Holly," he said, a frown creasing his forehead. "You think I'm still mourning Isabella, don't you? Well, I'm not. If you had researched me a bit more thoroughly before you came to Moscow you'd have stumbled on the truth—that my wife died in a car accident on her way to see her lover."

"But I...assumed..." Holly shook her head in bewilderment.

"That I was the grieving young husband solacing himself with beautiful women, his heart forever cold and buried with his first love." He was scornful, his eyes suddenly fierce.

"But the newspapers..."

"Got it wrong with a little help from my father-in-law." His smile was cold. "I went along with it because there were reputations at stake—to say nothing of Peter's legitimacy."

"Peter?" Holly stared up at him, feeling dull-witted and confused. "But surely it would be better if you told him he wasn't to blame for her death. He thinks he is responsible and that is why you don't love him. It's a terrible burden for a child to bear Dirk, surely you can see that."

He shrugged, his face full of bitterness. "Would he feel better if I also told him I'm not his father? I can even tell him his mother didn't know who his father was if you think that will help."

"But Peter is so like you," Holly burst out. Then, seeing the disbelief on his face, she added, "not in looks I admit, although I think his nose will be like yours when he's an adult, and he walks the same way; but in character he's exactly as you must have been thirty years ago."

"Don't try to make things better by pretending," he put her from him so that they stood apart, without touching, their hands hanging loosely at their sides.

"I'm not." Holly was emphatic. "There are a whole lot of things about him that are like you, but the most noticeable is his habit of making his eyes expressionless when he doesn't want anyone to know what he's thinking."

"My mother says the same." She heard a whisper of hope in his voice. "But I just thought she was trying to make me feel better by finding similarities that aren't really there."

Suddenly he reached out and took Holly in his arms again. "Do you really mean it? Is he like me?"

"I'd stake my life on it." Holly suddenly felt ridiculously lighthearted. Here was the explanation for Dirk's moody behaviour and his coldness towards Peter. It was, as she had surmised, a cover for his grief—but it was the sort of grief she could cope with. She banished Isabella to the back of her mind without compunction.

"He's your son, whatever your wife told you."

"How she must have hated me," Dirk shook his head, his eyes dark with anger. "My son, and I've let her almost destroy him, just as she destroyed our love."

His hands still hanging at his side, he explained. "I loved her very much, you know, even though our fathers more or less arranged the marriage when we were very young. I imagined roses and sunsets for ever. What I didn't know, what nobody knew, was that Isabella was a beautiful sham. Oh, she was well bred and suitably educated, but she had a desperate need for men. She fed on their admiration, enjoyed flaunting herself. It didn't even matter if I was there to witness it; in fact, she rather enjoyed making me jealous."

"And Peter?" Holly's eyes darkened with pain at the picture Dirk had just painted.

"Peter was a mistake." His grip tightened on her shoulders. "Isabella didn't intend to have children in case they spoiled her perfect figure, so from the moment he was born she set about proving that she was still attractive. All through her pregnancy I had hung onto the forlorn hope that having a baby to care for would change her. When it didn't, I became angry. It was then that she told me about all the affairs she had had, right from the first days of our marriage."

"And she told you that Peter wasn't yours?" Holly shook her head in disbelief, tears of sympathy trickling down her cheeks. "Why would she do that, Dirk, when he so obviously is?"

"Oh, I expect she intended to set the matter straight. She was probably punishing me for her pregnancy, for the fact that I had always wanted children. I should have known better than to believe her—goodness knows I had learned to discount most things she told me—but I suppose Peter was the final straw. While I was still reeling from the shock of it, she was killed. Her car went out of control and hit a tree."

He grabbed Holly's hands and held them tight. "Do you know how terrible it is to be glad that someone has died?"

"Yes, I do. The guilt is almost impossible to bear. It eats into you like a canker until in the end you feel that everything was your fault, that you willed them to die."

His anger faded as he stared at her, surprised by the quiet understanding in her voice.

130

"I was glad when my husband died." She told him. It was something she had hidden from herself until that moment. "He was cruel and sadistic because he was so crazy from drugs. I was frightened for my unborn baby. I didn't want him to know his father. I was wrong about that though."

Her eyes were full of remembered grief as she listened to her own admission. "Every child has the right to know their own parents. Perhaps Darren would have kicked the drugs if he had seen Martin...if he'd held him when he was a tiny, defenseless baby."

"What happened?" Dirk let go of her hands and pulled her to him.

"He died from a drug overdose." Suddenly Holly's voice was strong. At last she could face up to Martin's death, and her ambiguous feelings about Darren. "And Martin, my little boy, contracted leukemia when he was three. It took him nearly eighteen months to die and when he did, I wasn't there. I only left him for a short while because the doctors said I needed to rest, but I was wrong to listen to them. I should have stayed. I should have been there."

"Ah Holly, it's always easy to beat yourself up afterwards. I'm sure you were there for him when it mattered. His illness is why you left your job though." It was a statement, not a question, but Holly answered him anyway.

"Yes because I wanted to be with him all the time," she admitted, "but I asked my employers to keep it quiet because I didn't want the sort of media intrusion I'd had to live through when Darren died. I didn't want to see reporters every time I left the hospital. I didn't want the world waiting for my son to die."

Sudden enlightenment lifted the frown from Dirk's face. "Harwyn Williams! Of course, you were married to a famous singer, weren't you? Why didn't I remember that?"

"Because it was a long time ago. Darren died before Martin was born."

He gathered her close. "My poor darling, no wonder you often look so sad. Do you think you can ever learn to put it behind you and start again? I know Peter won't ever replace your own child, but he does need you—we both do." His voice was suddenly husky and Holly felt her heart lurch as his lips brushed her hair.

"I think I already have." She stared up at him, noticing for the first time the smooth, fine texture of his skin and the faint smattering of freckles across his nose.

"So have I." His hands were commanding against her back, forcing her ever closer. "Isabella taught me to distrust women and close relationships so well that I swore never to get emotionally involved with anyone ever again. I learned to separate need from love and played the field whenever it suited me. I thought I could treat you the same way, especially after you came on to me, but I couldn't. Your face kept invading my dreams, pricking at me like a burr so that I couldn't sleep, couldn't eat, couldn't think straight. I even began to drink—anything to block the fact that I was falling in love with you. And when I finally accepted my feelings, it was even worse. These past weeks have been hell, imagining you with Stephen, sure that you were playing some sort of game with both of us.

"And then the blow when Melina persuaded me that you were only here to write a juicy expose' about my supposedly amorous pursuits across the diplomatic world. That was the worst thing, the thought that you had deliberately deceived me; particularly as it seemed to fit in with your earlier flirtation."

Suddenly he frowned and shook her gently. "Just why did you flirt with me, Holly?"

"Because I couldn't bear what you were doing to Peter." She tilted her chin defiantly, noting his spark of remembered anger. "I thought if I flirted with you, you would want to spend time with both of us and by doing so you would learn how much he needed you."

"So my charms had nothing to do with it." He gave a wry chuckle. "That doesn't do very much for my ego, you know."

"I don't think your ego needs boosting," she retorted, her voice suddenly full of laughter. "In fact, it was your ego that frightened me off. It made me realise that I'd got in too far."

"This far, you mean?" He lowered his head, his mouth hovering a fraction away from hers.

"Yes." She closed her eyes, her body trembling under a sudden onslaught of emotion. For a moment they stood motionless, then, feeling Dirk's breath suddenly harsh on her cheek, her eyes snapped open again. He was staring at her, their faces inches apart.

"You're not playing with me, are you?" Her voice was strained. "You won't discard me, like all your other conquests. I won't become yesterday's news as far as Dirk Van Allen is concerned."

"I thought we had already agreed that we don't believe all we read in the newspapers," he teased her. Then his face softened.

"I'm sorry, Holly. Please don't look like that. You have no idea how much I love you? You're everything I ever wanted and never dreamed I would find. I think I fell in love with you the minute I saw you sitting at the breakfast table, trying to deal with Peter."

"But you were so horrid to me." Holly cast her mind back to her first day in Moscow, and tried to ignore the fact that Dirk was kissing the palm of her hand.

"That's because I was frightened by the instant effect you had on me. Despite everything that has been printed about me, Isabella's betrayal has left a scar, so I wasn't prepared to lay myself open to more pain. Then, when you began to flirt with me, I knew I was right. You were the same as Isabella, the same as all the women I have so casually used since she died."

"It didn't stop you from responding," she teased.

"That's because I'm not exactly a saint," he said with a wry grin. "But when you suddenly cooled off, I didn't know what to think, and Melina's story only made matters worse."

"And yet you were prepared to go to great lengths to save my reputation yesterday."

"And still am, provided it's only your public reputation." He pulled her close, so that their warmth intermingled and his fingers were points of fire on her back.

"Enough talking...I make it just under a million trillion kisses to go," he whispered. "And as you have this problem with bad dreams..."

"Not anymore." Holly shook her head as she told him why Martin's death had given her such nightmares.

"My poor darling." Suddenly Dirk swung her up into his arms and headed for his bedroom. "I'll make it up to you, I promise, although we may have to live through the gossip I tried to avoid, because after this evening I can't possibly pretend to a platonic friendship until we leave Moscow. But then we'll be back in London—and in London, who cares. Do you think you'll like being a diplomat's wife? The glamour is very much overrated, you know; it's often an endless round of functions, of trying to make small talk with people who speak very little English. It's also never, ever, for a moment, forgetting the responsibility of our position."

"Sounds like good writer's material to me." Holly tipped her face up to look at him, her hands clasped around his neck.

"Then you don't hanker after your old career?" He looked relieved.

She shook her head decisively. "No. That's part of my past, something I want to leave behind. But I do intend to write. I can't just be a wife."

"Nor would I want you to be." He cradled her closer. "That was one of the first things I liked about you—the way you are interested in everything around you, absorbing

134

yourself in Peter's games and Russian history with equal enthusiasm."

A bubble of laughter escaped Holly as she clung to him, adjusting her balance as he opened the door.

"What's so funny?" He looked down at her, his eyes quizzical.

"We are," Holly giggled. "This seduction scene is not exactly high romance, is it? We are so intent on the practical aspects of our life together, that we're not..."

"You speak for yourself." With a mock growl, Dirk pushed open the door with his foot, and tipped her onto the bed. Then he stripped off his shirt so that his skin gleamed pale in the lamplight. "I have every intention of giving the matter my complete concentration." His last words slurred as he bent and captured her mouth.

Much later, her body relaxed and warm and curled into the protection of Dirk's arms, Holly moved her head.

"Hello." He smiled at her, sleepy-eyed, his head tousled on the pillow. "I began to think that you were never going to wake up. In fact, I was beginning to consider the kiss Prince Charming used on Sleeping Beauty, if I remember my fairy tales correctly. Maybe I'll try it now, it's a shame to waste such a good idea."

He moved suddenly, tumbling the covers, pinning her to the mattress as he covered her with kisses, each one longer than the last.

"Don't, Dirk." She tried to push him away, her body already responding. "I want to ask you something."

"Practicalities again," he groaned, pausing for a moment. "This woman I've chosen talks too much."

"Please be serious," she begged, enjoying his teasing but needing an answer. "I just need to know why you called Peter your son before I told you how much he resembled you."

The laughter faded from Dirk's eyes and he rolled away from her, onto his back, and lay still, his face sombre. "I guess it was because I suddenly realised that it no longer mattered. He is accepted as my son by all the world, considers himself my son, and yet I was slowly destroying both of us with my own bitterness. I was ashamed too. Ashamed that despite everything I've done to him, he still loves me."

"You're his whole world so I'm glad you've learned to love him for himself, not just because you suddenly believe that he really is your son."

"I don't think I ever stopped loving him, not from the moment I first held him in my arms." Dirk gave a sad smile. "But he won't understand that. Will he ever learn to forgive me and trust me, Holly?"

"All he wants is your love. Forgiveness doesn't come into it." Holly slid her arms around his neck and held him tightly, sharing his sorrow for the wasted years of Peter's babyhood but sure of a happier future.

For a long moment they lay still, their bodies intertwined and passive as they comforted each other, then a teasing note crept into her voice as she shifted slightly.

"There's only one thing Peter will be disappointed about," she said, her eyes firmly fixed on a point above Dirk's left ear.

"And that is?" He propped himself up on his elbow, a slight frown creasing his forehead.

"The fact that we don't need to sleep in the same bed now that my bad dreams are cured." She shrieked as he began to tickle her, but within moments she was making tiny moaning noises as Dirk's tickling became a caress.

"You're a witch." He caught her face between his hands and kissed her gently. "And you will never, ever need to leave my bed because you'll never leave my heart."

Epilogue

It was nearly five months later that a taxi drew up outside a mews cottage on the outskirts of London.

"Is this it?" Peter hopped about excitedly on the pavement while Dirk paid the taxi driver. He was almost an inch taller and his cheeks were rosy and tanned from the Moscow summer.

"This is it." Holly produced a key. "Go and open the front door while Daddy and I carry the cases in."

"Which is my room?" Peter was already halfway down the path. "I want to see my room first."

"Your room is at the top of the stairs," Holly replied, picking up a small suitcase. "You will need to unlock the door."

She followed him into the house and heard his gasp of pleasure as he opened the bedroom door. When she climbed the stairs a few minutes later, he was unpacking a box of cars from Martin's cupboard, adding them to the ones already littering the carpet.

He smiled up at her. "You didn't tell me about the toys."

She leaned her head against Dirk's shoulder as he came up behind her. "I kept the door was locked because they used to belong to a very special little boy, and I was keeping them safe until I found another special little boy to give them to."

Peter stared at her for a moment and then lunged at her knees, hugging them briefly before returning to his game.

"I love you." His voice was matter-of-fact, without sentiment. "Will you tell me about the other little boy?"

"At bedtime," Holly promised, and then Dirk's arms were tight about her, pulling her against him as he silently expressed his understanding.

"I love you too," he whispered, "and I want to see what treats are in my bedroom!"

"Damp sheets and full suitcases," Holly protested as he drew her gently away from the door. "What about Peter?"

"Peter is absorbed in a very complicated game that will keep him occupied for a long time." He led her along the passageway to the master bedroom, and locked the door behind them.

"Now Holly Van Allen," he said, taking her in his arms, "Don't you think it's about time you welcomed me into your home?"

The end

Other Books We Love books by Sheila Claydon:

Contemporary Romance
Cabin Fever
Reluctant Date
Double Fault
Kissing Maggie Silver
Mending Jodie's Heart - When Paths Meet Book 1
Finding Bella Blue - When Paths Meet Book 2
Saving Katy Gray - When Paths Meet Book 3
Miss Locatelli
Remembering Rose - Mapleby Memories Book 1
The Sheila Claydon Special Edition

Vintage Romance
Bouquet of Thorns
The Hollywood Collection

In the 1980s Sheila Claydon wrote several romances under the pseudonym Anne Beverley. Then a busy career and family life got in the way and before she knew it she had turned her back on the characters who were begging to be liberated from her imagination. Now she is back to writing fiction again and, considerably older and no longer shy, writes under her own name.

Her motto is a quote by the late Ray Bradbury: *"First, find out what your hero wants. Then just follow him."*

Although family remains central to her life, she still finds the time to read, to write, and to travel. Many of the places she has visited feature in her books. Her fans say that reading them is like buying a ticket to romance.

You can find her at

https://www.facebook.com/SheilaClaydon.author/

www.ingramcontent.com/pod-product-compliance
Lightning Source LLC
Chambersburg PA
CBHW060427260626
47161CB00005B/1812

* 9 7 8 1 7 7 3 6 2 5 8 4 3 *